THE WEDDING CHALLENGE

*Chased to the altar—three independent cousins swept off
their feet by the most eligible Englishmen!*

Pepper, Izzy and **Jemima Jane** are cousins—with
nothing in common except the gorgeous red hair
they've inherited from their grandmother! They even
grew up on different continents: Pepper is heiress to
an American business empire, Izzy and JJ shared their
very English childhood as adopted sisters....

But do they have more in common than they realize?

For the first time in their lives, the three cousins find
themselves together: as a family, as friends, as
business partners. And they're about to discover that
they're not so different from each other after all!

Pepper, Izzy and JJ are thoroughly modern women,
determined to be ruled by the head, not the heart.
Now their lives are turned upside down as each meets
a man who challenges them to let love into their
lives—with dramatic consequences!

This month Pepper has an unexpected encounter in
The Independent Bride.
Look out for Izzy's story in *The Accidental Mistress*
and JJ's in *The Duke's Proposal.*

Dear Reader,

This book was born in a wine bar. I was with two friends who I really thought had got life sussed. Then a smoky-voiced singer started singing about fields of barley, and we all went quiet. Yes, we could run our lives, pay our bills, have fun. But….

Modern women can handle anything. Well, that's what we tell ourselves. Most of the time it's true, too. But when you're in love you're on your own in a strange country without a compass. And everyone else looks as if they know exactly what they're doing.

Cousins Pepper, Izzy and Jemima Jane are young, vibrant, successful—and when love strikes it doesn't make a blind bit of difference. Though they're not admitting it, of course. Especially not to each other!

I really love these women. And I sympathize with them. Been there, done that; still wince when I think about some of it. And I am so glad they get their happy ending. Hope you are, too!

Best wishes

Sophie Weston

SOPHIE WESTON
The Independent Bride

The Wedding Challenge

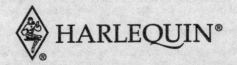

TORONTO • NEW YORK • LONDON
AMSTERDAM • PARIS • SYDNEY • HAMBURG
STOCKHOLM • ATHENS • TOKYO • MILAN • MADRID
PRAGUE • WARSAW • BUDAPEST • AUCKLAND

ISBN 0-373-03747-3

THE INDEPENDENT BRIDE

First North American Publication 2003.

This edition published by arrangement with Harlequin Books S.A.

Visit us at www.eHarlequin.com

Printed in U.S.A.

PROLOGUE

THE last of the overnight flights out of JFK to London was about to board. The departure lounge was crowded to overflowing, but even so one alert journalist was scanning the faces carefully. Rewarded, he caught his breath with excitement.

He nudged his companion in the ribs. 'Did you see who that was?'

The companion was a generation older than the keen young television correspondent; it took a lot to get him excited. Besides, he had made a career out of not being impressed by anyone. 'If you mean Steven Konig, I saw him on the main concourse.'

The younger man swung round. 'Really? Konig—the food for famine guy? He's here? Where?'

'They boarded him first,' said the other, bored.

'Oh, *that's* who it was! I thought it must be royalty.' The younger man had a point to prove, too. 'You do know it was the top brass escorting him?'

His companion got even more bored. 'If you mean David Guber, he and Konig go way back. They were students at Oxford together.'

That would silence the upstart, he thought.

But it didn't. Amazingly, the younger man's chagrin lasted only a few seconds before he was bouncing back, eager as a puppy.

'I didn't catch Konig, but I did catch someone a lot more interesting.' He paused expectantly.

The older man yawned.

'The Tiger Cub,' said up-and-coming television financial

newsman tantalisingly. And sat back, waiting to be asked 'Who or what is the Tiger Cub?'

It did not come.

It would be too much to say that the older man sat bolt upright and looked keenly round the lounge. Excitement, after all, was not his bag. But there was no doubt his journalist's antennae twitched.

'The Calhoun girl?' he said, after a moment.

'Pepper Calhoun, yes,' said his companion, disappointed but still fighting. At least he knew that Penelope Anne Calhoun was called Pepper by her intimates.

The older man stared into the middle distance, his eyes narrowed. 'That's interesting,' he said at last.

'Yes, that's what I thought. Do you think Calhoun Carter are going on the acquisition trail in the UK? I can think of a couple of retail companies ripe for acquisition.' He smacked his lips at the thought, especially as he could be the first back to London with the news. At least, he could if Sandy Franks was as indifferent as he seemed.

But Sandy Franks was still thinking aloud. 'The last I heard, the girl wasn't working for Calhoun Carter. Mary Ellen Calhoun has been telling people that her granddaughter is going to gain experience in the outside world before coming back into the company for good.'

'You believe that?'

'It's possible.' He sucked his teeth, pondering. 'Maybe Pepper Calhoun has decided to do her own thing. Visit the sights. Have a fling with the boyfriend. What is she? Twenty-six? Twenty-seven? She's got a right to party a bit before she settles down to a life of corporate greed.'

'*The Tiger Cub?*' Young and eager Martin Tammery laughed heartily at the naïveté of experience. 'She doesn't party. Her idea of a good time is an eighteen-hour day topped off by a night of conference calls. And she hasn't had a boyfriend since business school.'

'Then she'll be ripe for a romantic interlude,' said experience with conviction.

His companion stayed unconvinced. 'The one thing that is absolutely certain about Pepper Calhoun is that she doesn't *do* romance. Never has. Never will.'

'How can you be sure?'

'She's going to inherit one of the retail giants. I've been keeping a file on her since she went to her first prom. Believe me, she is her grandmother's heir in every way there is. Brain like a computer, tongue like a razor, heart like outer space.'

The older man blinked. 'Run that past me again? What's outer space got to do with Pepper Calhoun?'

'They're both cold and empty,' said the other with feeling. 'And totally inaccessible.'

CHAPTER ONE

WHAT a difference a week makes!

Penelope Anne Calhoun rested her tired red head against the wall of the departure lounge and tried to be philosophical.

Exactly a week ago today she had thought she was nicely on track for the rest of her life. She'd had friends she trusted, a new project she believed in, and the best address in New York.

There had been just the one tiny cloud on the horizon, and Pepper had been sure she could deal with that. Well, eventually. When she had to. When the final funding for *Out of the Attic* was in place and she could go to her grandmother and say, This is what I'm going to do.

It was not as if they hadn't tried to warn her.

'Pepper, are you sure this is a good idea?' her old mentor from business school had asked. 'I mean—concept shopping! Love the idea. But what happens when your grandmother finds out?'

And she said, so airily, so positively, 'Nothing will happen.'

She could see the professor was dubious. 'Are you sure of that?'

And she was. She was. 'Absolutely,' Pepper said with total assurance.

'Mrs Calhoun won't see it as a rival to Calhoun Carter?'

Pepper laughed heartily. 'CC has branches in every major city in the US and five overseas countries. Beside CC, *Out of the Attic* is a minnow. No—less than a minnow. It's plankton to a whale.'

'That's not quite what I meant,' said her teacher dryly. 'I was thinking more of a rival suitor.'

And, heaven help her, she had even laughed at that.

'Okay. Maybe she'll kick up a little at first. But she'll see it my way eventually. She knows I have to prove myself.'

'Does she?'

'Yup,' Pepper had said, with the total confidence of a woman who had been Mary Ellen Calhoun's little princess since she was eight. 'My grandmother wants what's best for me. You see, she loves me.'

The guy hadn't said any more. Pepper had felt quite sorry for him, out-argued by his own pupil like that. She had taken him out to a spectacular gourmet dinner to make it up to him.

And how wrong she had been. How wrong.

She first realised that things weren't going to plan the day that Ed kidnapped her.

She wasn't scared. Of course she wasn't. She had known Ed Ivanov all her life. Anyway, Calhouns didn't scare easy. Pepper was a Calhoun right the way through to that cool business brain of hers.

So she kept her head and stayed calm.

'What's this about, Ed?'

But he just shook his head. The noise in the helicopter made a great excuse.

Pepper looked down at unfamiliar rolling countryside and tried to guess where they were. A long way from New York by now. Ed had got her into the 'copter, saying he wanted her to meet some potential investors. Ed was one of the tiny group of trusted friends who knew about *Out of the Attic*. So she'd gone with him without a second thought.

By the time they were well out of the metropolitan area, following a river valley, she was having second thoughts all right. Ed hadn't mentioned investors again. In fact Ed wasn't talking much at all.

When Pepper had walked off with the Year Prize at business school, it had been for a paper on problem solving. So she said to herself, *Right, Pepper, solve this*.

She tapped him on the arm, and when he turned mouthed

at him carefully, 'There are only three reasons for you to do this. Ransom. Ungovernable passion. You've gone mad. Which is it?'

But he waved a hundred-dollar manicure to indicate the noise of the rotor arms and did not answer.

Pepper shook her head. Unless he had been fired in the last twenty-four hours, Ed did not need money. He was a successful Wall Street analyst. And the idea of passion was laughable. They had dated briefly at business school but it had ended peaceably and neither of them had a broken heart.

Or, Ed's beach readings, she remembered, ran to highly coloured adventure stories. Maybe he was whisking her off for a secret weekend as a prelude to another proposal of marriage? She looked at him. He was peering at the valley below the helicopter, nibbling at a nail.

Romantic? Ed? Nah!

She considered him from under her long lashes. They were surprisingly dark compared with her flame-red hair. One of her few good points, she always said. Pepper was realistic about her lack of attractions.

Which was another reason why she didn't think passion had driven Ed to enforced seduction. He did not look at her. He did not touch her. In fact, he was behaving more like a transcontinental courier with an awkward package than a man in love.

Anyway, surely even Ed wouldn't think that kidnapping a woman was a good way to persuade her to marry him?

And then the helicopter came down in the middle of a clearing and Ed started talking again.

'This is my father's fishing cabin,' he said and helped her out.

Keep it light, she told herself. *Keep it light.* 'Since when do I fish?'

He did not look mad. He gave her a slightly harassed smile. 'We're just up here for a meeting. I told you.'

That was when Pepper started to get a really bad feeling about the trip.

She hid it. 'Do I need my visual aids?' she said dryly. She had brought all the stuff with her for a really great presentation of *Out of the Attic*.

He shook his head.

'Somehow, you don't surprise me,' she said with irony. 'Okay. Lead on.'

It was really quite a simple cabin—single storey, in need of repair. The way down to it was full of puddles, too. Her shiny black city pumps, discreetly plain and shockingly expensive, were never going to be the same again. Still, at least she didn't take a tumble—unlike Ed.

Rain dripped through the trees. It soaked Pepper's hair until the elegant auburn pleat turned black and flattened on the top of her head. It darkened the shoulders of her designer label navy jacket. She felt an uncomfortable trickle down the neck of her pearl silk blouse. But it wasn't the spring rain that sent chills up and down her spine.

'If the CIA are trying to recruit me, you can tell them now—no dice.'

But it was not the CIA, any more than it was the non-existent investors. Or Ed in romantic excess.

It was someone who was coming out onto the rough stoop at the sound of their approach.

It was her grandmother.

All desire to find humour in the situation left Pepper abruptly. She stopped dead. The look she turned on Ed was hot enough to melt asbestos.

Bad conscience made Ed peevish. 'No need to be so dramatic. It's just business.'

Pepper was very pale. 'No, Ed. It's my *life*.'

He looked down his nose. 'Now you're talking like a teen queen.'

She looked back at the cabin. Mary Ellen Calhoun was watching them attentively. Even in the wet spring woods she was wearing Paris design and diamonds. Pepper saw the gleam of Venetian earrings under her grandmother's cap of skilfully tinted dark hair. Mary Ellen Calhoun was seventy-three but she would go to her grave a brunette.

Pepper said, 'What did my grandmother promise you to get me here?'

He looked genuinely shocked. 'Nothing. She just wanted me to stop you making a big mistake.'

'It's a mistake to back my own idea? I thought that was why we went to business school.'

'Look, Pepper,' he said patiently, '*Out of the Attic* is a retail start-up. That's five years of your life, minimum. Mary Ellen doesn't want to wait five years to get you back on board at Calhoun Carter.'

'Since when do you call her Mary Ellen? You been talking to her a lot recently, Ed?'

He winced. 'Not really. We—er—bumped into each other at a charity reception a couple of weeks ago...'

'My grandmother doesn't go to charity receptions for fun,' said Pepper dispassionately. 'And she never bumps into anyone.'

He looked at her, half-defiant, half-ashamed. Pepper squared her shoulders.

'Oh, well, it had to happen some time, I guess. Wait here,' she told Ed quietly. 'This is not going to be pretty.'

The moment she came face to face with her grandmother Pepper knew what was going to happen. One look and she just *knew*.

It was there, in Mary Ellen's black currant eyes. Mary Ellen wanted the last of the Calhouns back on the board. Like *now*.

Not that you could tell that from her behaviour. Mary Ellen came forward, hands out, smiling, just as she always did. Glutinously innocent. Pepper had learned to distrust that innocence the way she would distrust a basking snake.

Of course, Mary Ellen was not your average grandmother. She had been President of Calhoun Carter since her husband had died thirty-three years ago. That sort of thing gave you an edge. Pepper might distrust her, but she respected her, too. And she was realising that she was fighting for her life.

She did not take the hands held out to her. She said quietly, 'Hello, Grandmother.'

Mary Ellen looked startled. It was a voice she did not recognise.

Not surprising, thought Pepper. She didn't recognise it herself.

'It's good to see you, honey,' Mary Ellen said in her soft, deceptive, ladylike tones.

'No, it isn't. It's business,' said Pepper grimly. 'Spare me the fancy stuff. Get on with it.'

The two women's eyes locked.

Then Mary Ellen gave the tinkling laugh she had perfected in the days when she was a popular debutante; before she'd married her way out of impoverished gentility; before she'd hijacked her husband's company and became a ruthless tycoon.

'Then you'd better come in out of the rain,' she said with a charming pout.

'And Ed?' Pepper was mocking. 'Do you want him in out of the rain as well?'

Mary Ellen frowned. 'He's a man. A little rain won't kill him.'

'Thought you wouldn't want any witnesses.' Pepper nodded.

Mary Ellen did not deign to answer that. She stalked inside like an empress. And the moment the door closed behind her granddaughter she abandoned innocence, ladylike charm and the pout all in one go. Suddenly she looked what she was, thought Pepper. Seventy-three years old and mean as a snake.

Pepper drew a deep breath. 'Okay. Fire away. I can see that you've heard about *Out of the Attic*. What do you think can do to stop me?'

Mary Ellen smiled. 'I've already done it.'

'Excuse me?'

'Really, you are such a child. I told the finance department to put it around that anyone who lent money to you could kiss goodbye to Carter Calhoun business. For ever.'

Pepper went very still. 'I see. I suppose they were doing that this morning? That's why you had Ed get me out of town? So I wouldn't be there if anyone wanted to call me to check?'

Mary Ellen shrugged. 'What's to check?'

But Pepper knew she was right. Mary Ellen had made sure Pepper was out of the way when the news broke in case she found a way to fight back.

'You always did fight dirty,' Pepper said. 'Why didn't I remember that?'

Mary Ellen was impatient. 'I want you back in the firm. You know that. This little idea of yours is just a waste of time.' She opened her electronic organiser. 'Shall we say—middle of next week? That will give you time to move out of that nasty apartment and get yourself home, where you belong. I'll tell Jim to organise you an office.'

'No,' said Pepper quietly.

Mary Ellen extracted the stylus and tapped in a deliberate note. 'Seven forty-five on Wednesday,' she said, as if Pepper hadn't spoken. 'Go to the plant and ask for Connie. She's the Human Resources Manager now. She'll find—'

Pepper raised her voice. 'I said *no.*'

The inside of the cabin was very dusty, but Mary Ellen had cleaned up a corner for herself. Typically it was the best chair in the room. And it was set at the desk. She sat down now and steepled her fingertips.

'You don't have a choice,' she said calmly. 'Your little business is a busted flush. Who else but me would employ you?'

Pepper stared. Her thoughts whirled like a rising storm.

I thought she loved me. She doesn't. She just loves making everyone dance to her tune. How on earth did I miss that?

It hurt. It really hurt.

'Let me spell it out for you,' said Mary Ellen. She sounded almost motherly.

That truly sickened Pepper. For a moment she could not speak.

Mary Ellen misunderstood her silence. Mary Ellen thought she had won. But then Mary Ellen always did win.

'Look at it this way. You're the last Calhoun. Anyone in the retail business is going to think you're a spy. A business in any other sector will just think you have to be a liability or you'd be in the family firm where you belong. It's a no-brainer.'

Pepper was shaking. 'A no-brainer,' she agreed with heavy irony.

Mary Ellen gave her famously charming, naughty child smile. 'Sure,' she agreed. 'Glad you see it so clearly. Your little idea is dead. You won't get funding from anyone in North America.' She tapped the organiser. 'See you Wednesday.'

Pepper drew a deep breath. Get a grip, she told herself feverishly, get a grip. Lose your temper and she's won. She already thinks she's won. This is your last chance...

And she said quietly, 'No.'

She was right. Mary Ellen had been quite sure that she had won. She did not believe that Pepper would hold out. Startled, furious, disbelieving, she went on the attack. Mary Ellen Calhoun on the attack did not take prisoners.

Pepper just stood there, under an assault of words like hailstones. In the end they all came back to the same point. Pepper was Calhoun Carter Industries' property, bought and paid for over years. The very best education money could buy had seen to that. Along with the house in the South of France, the condo in New York, the South Sea Island mountain retreat, her suite in the Calhoun mansion...

Pepper hung on to cool reason but it was an effort. 'But they aren't *mine*.'

Mary Ellen showed her teeth in a shark's smile. 'Got it at last!'

Oh, Pepper got it. Slowly. Reluctantly. With disbelief. But she got it.

'You mean that all the stuff you've given me over the years—'

'Invested,' corrected Mary Ellen coldly. 'You are an investment. Nothing more.'

If Pepper had been pale before, she was ashen now. This was the woman who had introduced her at parties as 'my little princess'?

Mary Ellen smiled. 'Think about it. The European schools. The year in Paris. Seed corn. I even arranged for you to go to business school five years younger than everyone else, so you wouldn't want time out when the company needed you.'

Pepper was outraged. 'The business school took me on my own merits. I won a *prize*, for God's sake.'

Mary Ellen mocked that, too. 'Problem solving! When did you ever solve a problem? All your problems have been bought off by Calhoun money.'

That was when Mary Ellen listed them. Not just the right schools, the right clothes, the right apartments, the right friends. The senior businessmen who had taken her calls and talked to her like an equal. The junior businessmen who had dated her…

Dated…?

Pepper gulped. Her blouse was not just damp and cold any more. It was icy. A cascade of icicles was thundering down her spine. She was shivering so much she could hardly speak.

'What do you mean? What have my dates got to do with this?'

Mary Ellen saw that she had scored a hit. Her eyes gleamed.

'You have no idea what it cost me to get you a social life,' she went on with that trill of laughter that was her trademark. It was very musical, very ladylike. But the eyes that met Pepper's across the dusty old cabin were not ladylike in the least.

Even so—*dated?*

'You're nothing but a potato,' said Mary Ellen, light and

cruel and suddenly horribly believable. 'Who would bother with you if you weren't my grandchild?'

Pepper was the first to admit that she was not fashionably slender, but she had always thought she was good company. That her friends liked her for that. She said so.

Mary Ellen's hard little eyes snapped. 'And I suppose you think that one day you'll meet Prince Charming and get married, too? Grow up!'

'I'm sorry?'

'You have only one chance to be a bride,' said Mary Ellen, showing her teeth like a shark. 'And that's if I buy you a husband. After all those mercy dates I paid for, I've got a good long list of candidates.'

That was when Pepper knew that she could not take any more. There was no point in even trying. With a superhuman effort, she told her icy muscles to stop shaking and *move*. And she walked out.

Mary Ellen was not expecting it. 'Where are you going?' she yelled, suddenly not even pretending to be ladylike any more.

Pepper did not stop. She went running, scrambling up the soggy path, to where Ed was sitting.

Her grandmother ran after her, but halted at the point where the path began to climb.

'You get back here this minute,' she yelled.

Pepper did not stop. Not even when she fell to one knee. Not even when she felt her pantyhose tear and blood trickle down her shin. She didn't care. She didn't care about anything but getting away from the grandmother whose affection had been a lie right from the start.

By the time she reached Ed, she was panting. 'Take me back to New York,' she said. 'Take me back *now*.'

He hesitated, but only for a moment. It would have taken a braver man than Ed Ivanov to face Mary Ellen in this mood. He took Pepper's arm and hurried her towards the clearing where the helicopter was waiting.

Ladylike, five foot two, Mary Ellen had a voice like a bass drum when roused. It reached them easily. So did the fury.

'You'll never make it on your own, Penelope Anne Calhoun, do you hear me? I *own* you.'

A week later, Pepper knew exactly how true that was. So she leaned against the wall, skulking down as a party of VIPs swept onto the London plane in advance of everyone else. She did not care about VIPs, but there was an outside chance that they might recognise her. After all, Mary Ellen was a VIP. As the Calhoun heir, Pepper had been one too for most of her life.

Well, that was all over now. A good thing, too, she told herself.

She would get to London. She would put together a new life. And she would survive.

All she had to do was keep clear of VIPs.

'Professor Konig?' The flight attendant had obviously been waiting for them. She was instantly alert, full of professional smiles. 'Welcome on board, sir. This way.'

The VIP and the airline director followed her.

'So that's what you get in first class,' Steven Konig muttered to David Guber. 'Instant name-check and personal escort to your seat.'

The attendant took his jacket and the ticket stub to label it, and left her boss to do the formal farewells. Steven looked after her.

'Is it enough to justify the cost, I ask myself?'

The other man smiled. 'You old Puritan! Still working on the principle I'm uncomfortable therefore I am?'

Steven laughed. 'You may be right.'

Dave punched his arm lightly. 'You're important enough to fly the Atlantic without having your knees under your nose any more, Steven. Live with it.'

'Can I quote you?' Steven was dry.

Dave Guber was not only a long-standing friend, he was a main board member of this airline. He grinned, 'If you do, I'll sue.' He shook hands and added soberly, 'I mean it. I'm really grateful, Steven. You saved our butts.'

Steven shook his head, disclaiming.

'Yes, you did. If you hadn't come through for me we'd have had a conference and no keynote speaker. Great speech, too.'

Steven shrugged. 'I was glad to do it. I've wanted to do a think piece on the subject for a long time.'

'Yeah, sure. Like you haven't got enough to fill your time already.'

'No, I mean it,' Steven insisted. 'It makes a change.' He gave a rueful smile. 'It seems like all I do these days is meetings, meetings, meetings. It was really nice just to sit down and *think* for once.'

Dave Guber looked quizzical. 'Wish you were only doing one job again?'

'Chairman of Kplant is my *job*,' Steven told him drily. 'Being Master of Queen Margaret's isn't a job; it's a vocation. Ask the Dean.'

They both grinned. They understood each other perfectly. They had first met at Queen Margaret's College, Oxford, as students years ago. And they had both been fined by the Dean regularly for standard student bad behaviour.

Dave cocked an eyebrow. 'He isn't glad to see you back?'

'Spitting tintacks,' agreed Steven, amused.

'That must make life peaceful.'

'Hey, if I wanted peace I'd have stayed in the lab. You say goodbye to peace the moment you open your own company.'

Dave's career had been with big international corporates. He looked at his friend curiously. 'Is it worth it?'

'It's great,' said Steven. There was no mistaking his enthusiasm.

'You never want to slow down?' Dave asked tentatively.

Slowing down was heresy in business, of course. But he

remembered the gorgeous blonde whom Steven had dated all those years ago. No one mentioned her any more. Nobody linked his name with anyone else, either. Dave thought he had never met anyone as lonely as Steven Konig.

'Do you never think about—er—a family, maybe?'

Steven's face changed. He didn't frown exactly. He just withdrew—very slightly, very politely. Suddenly Dave wasn't talking to his old buddy any more. He was taking formal leave of an international figure.

Dave sighed and gave up.

'Well, don't forget you're going to come and stay with us the very next vacation you get. Marise and I are counting on it.'

Vacation? Steven managed to repress a hollow laugh.

'Sure thing,' he said. It was vague enough not to count as a promise. Steven always kept his promises, so he didn't hand them out lightly.

'I'll hold you to that.'

Steven gave his sudden smile, the one that made him look just like the student who had once worked out how to set off fireworks by remote control from Queen Margaret's venerable tower. His eyes were vivid with amusement.

'I'll put it in the five-year plan.'

Dave flung up his hands in mock despair. 'You're crazy.'

'You said it yourself. I'm a Big Name,' Steven said crisply. 'For that, there's a price.'

David Guber was an important man, with stock options and the power to hire and fire. But he wasn't Steven Konig, who had single-handedly taken his food research business from the small companies sector to the big time. The press fell over themselves to interview Steven Konig in five continents. Of course there was going to be a price.

Dave sighed. 'Well, if you ever get off the carousel come see us,' he said. And to the glamorous flight attendant, who still hovered, 'Make sure Professor Konig has the journey of his life. We owe this man, big time.' He pumped his hand again. 'You're a great guy, Steven. Have a good flight.'

Steven was already opening his briefcase before Guber had left the plane.

'Can I get you anything, Professor?' the attendant asked.

Steven bit back a wry smile. So Dave Guber thought he ought to date, did he? How was a man to do that when every woman he met called him Professor? Or Chairman? Or even, God help him, Master?

'A drink?' The flight attendant knew her duty to the friend of a boss so big she had only ever seen him on video before. 'Coffee?'

Steven gave her his ordinary smile, the one he used when more than half his mind was elsewhere. 'No, thank you.'

'A warm towel?' pressed the flight attendant, trying hard.

'Nothing.' He corrected that. 'You'll give me everything I need if you just keep other people away.'

He had caught sight of several British delegates from the conference in the airport. He could just see them grabbing the chance of a transatlantic flight to buttonhole him. Experience had taught him that someone always wanted advice they didn't listen to or the name of contacts whom they misused.

He said with feeling, 'I'd really appreciate some peace.'

'You've got it,' said the flight attendant, relieved.

Steven worked until long after the attendants had put out the cabin lights and his fellow passengers had composed themselves for sleep. He finished making notes on the monthly statements of Kplant, dictated two memos and a letter, and then skimmed the agenda for the next college meeting. Finishing that, he looked at his watch. Space for two hours' sleep if he was sensible.

And I'm always sensible, thought Steven wryly. With two jobs, three titles and more responsibilities than he could shake a stick at, he had to be.

He stretched out on the wonder of a first-class transcontinental airline bed and clicked off his overhead light. He was asleep in seconds.

*   *   *

Pepper had never flown coach before. It was an experience, she thought grimly.

The seat was uncomfortably tight. The woman in the next seat kept jabbing her in the ribs and maintained an agitated monologue until she finally fell asleep. And in the row behind a party of young entrepreneurs were drinking and laughing loudly about some conference they had been to in New York. By the time the cabin crew had finally settled them down Pepper knew that sleep was hopeless.

Suppose that's the price of running away, she told herself, with an attempt at humour. No more business class for you.

Only it didn't make her laugh. Not even smile. In fact she felt her stomach clench as if she had just swallowed a glassful of ice. And not because of the loss of luxury.

I am not running away. I am *not* running away.

Pepper winced. Even in her head she sounded defensive.

Who are you kidding, Pepper? Of course you're running away!

She shivered—then pulled the thin flight blanket up to her chin. It made her feel a bit warmer but it did not stop the inner turmoil.

She had always known that crossing her grandmother was a risk. But she had never suspected the lengths that Mary Ellen would go to.

Because I still thought I was her little princess! I thought she loved me. What an idiot I was. What a blind, naïve idiot. And I thought I was so street-smart!

Mary Ellen's revenge had not been subtle. It had been *fast*.

Within two days of their secret meeting Pepper had notice to quit her apartment. Well, she had expected that; her grandmother had rented it to her in the first place. She had not expected to find her appointment diary suddenly emptying. Or the company that rented her office space suddenly demanding that she pay a year's rent up-front or leave in a week. Or to have her platinum credit card suddenly withdrawn.

She had tried to speak to Mary Ellen. But her grandmother

had refused to take her calls. So Pepper had gone to the Calhoun Carter building.

Mary Ellen refused to see her. More, she'd kept her waiting for half an hour, then had the security force escort her from the building under guard.

Pepper had not believed it. *'Why?'* she had said to Mary Ellen's PA. She had known Carmen all her life.

Carmen had tears in her eyes but she did not stop the uniformed guards.

'Everyone will think I've been stealing from her,' Pepper said, still too bewildered to be indignant.

Carmen looked as if she were going to cry in earnest. 'That's why.'

'You mean—' Pepper struggled with it. 'This is a publicity stunt?'

'Mrs Calhoun says you want independence, you've got it.' Carmen sounded as if she had learned it off by heart. And as if she were eating glass.

'You mean she wants to destroy my credibility,' said Pepper slowly. 'Oh, Carmen!'

The PA blew her nose. 'Better go quietly, Pepper. You don't want to make the evening news.'

So Pepper went.

She went back to her apartment, sat down and made a list of what she had got going for her. It was frighteningly little— a good business brain, a wardrobe of executive suits, enough money to live for six months if she was careful, and the ability to speak three languages. Oh, and a really good project in *Out of the Attic*. Only her grandmother was going to make sure that *Out of the Attic* never came to market.

She was packing when the doorbell rang. She checked through the spy hole. *Ed?*

She opened the door. 'What do you want, Ed?' she said wearily.

He divested himself of his overcoat and sat down on the sofa, taking her with him. He took her hand and held onto it.

Pepper snatched it back. 'You don't have to look like that. Nobody died.'

But Ed went on looking honest and remorseful.

'Not yet. But your career is damn nearly gone,' he said frankly. 'Why don't you make it up with Mary Ellen? It's crazy to throw away Calhoun Carter for a whim. You were born for business.'

Pepper flinched. 'And not for Prince Charming,' she said savagely.

Ed was disconcerted. 'What?'

She took a deep breath. 'Will you tell me something, Ed?'

'If I can.'

'When we went out together—was I a mercy date?'

He hesitated just a fraction too long.

So her grandmother had not lied. Pepper had hoped against hope that it was one of Mary Ellen's snaky tricks. But clearly it was the simple truth.

'Thank you,' she said quietly. 'Goodbye, Ed.'

It was a night when Pepper despaired. She had never felt more lonely in her life.

It was also the night that she decided. She had to go somewhere nobody would care that she was Mary Ellen Calhoun's granddaughter. And if that looked like running away, tough.

She put her life in order faster than she would have believed possible. She got rid of furniture. Gave away her books and CDs. Said goodbye to the two or three people who would care and was out of the apartment before Mary Ellen could send in someone in uniform to evict her.

So this was where she found out whether she deserved her prize for problem solving, Pepper thought wryly now, as one by one even the partying entrepreneurs in the row behind fell asleep.

If she did, she would survive in London. She would set up *Out of the Attic* in England instead of the States.

And find Prince Charming?

Pepper closed her eyes. No need to get over-ambitious,

she told herself. I think you can say goodbye to that one. There, at least, Mary Ellen had proved to be right.

And I never want another mercy date if I live to be a hundred.

In the first-class section, Steven Konig came awake the moment the smell of coffee began to waft through the cabin. Everyone else was still slumbering under doused lights. But the flight attendant saw him stir. She came over.

'Professor?'

He sat up, rubbing his eyes.

'It starts with my alarm call now, does it?'

She was bewildered. 'I'm sorry, Professor?'

Steven said wearily, 'Could you just lay off Professoring me until I've had my orange juice?'

She did not understand. 'No need to move just yet if you don't want to, sir,' she said softly. 'We've got more than an hour until we land.'

He smiled at her, shaking himself free of the airline blankets and pillows. 'No, that's fine. I've got work to do. And I always like to see the sunrise.'

She nodded and went back to her galley. No one else in the business class cabin stirred. The smell of coffee intensified.

When did I last wake up to the smell of coffee? Steven thought. That holiday in Tuscany with the Cooper family when I'd just got the Chair of Business Innovation? Five years ago? Six? Become a success—give up someone making you coffee in the morning!

He gave a dry smile and ran his hand over his chin. He had a heavy beard. Years ago, Courtney had told him that she went to bed with Don Juan and woke up with the Pirate King. That was when she'd still been in his life and they were laughing about their secret love affair. Before she'd decided that rich kid Tom Underwood was a better bet than a man who had to put himself through his PhD as a petrol pump attendant. It hadn't mattered to Courtney that Tom was his best friend. But then it hadn't mattered to Courtney that Steven loved her, either.

Well, all that was a long time ago. These days he tried to look like a smooth businessman at all times. He went to the softly lit first-class bathroom to freshen up.

But on the point of shaving off the morning's beard he stopped. He'd been on duty at that damned conference for over a week. All that time he had been shaving twice a day, listening to boring papers, making small talk with elliptical officials and never, ever exchanging a word with anyone that wasn't about business. He was tired of *behaving*.

Arrested, Steven considered his mirrored image. He ran a thoughtful hand over the dark stubble. He looked like a gun-slinger in an old movie, he thought, amused. Not a chairman. Never a master of an Oxford college. Above all not a professor. No one who met him for the first time today would think of calling him Professor.

'Go for it,' he told himself.

He put on a clean shirt but left it hanging defiantly outside his trousers. The piratical look would give the perfect flight attendant a shock, he thought. *Excellent!*

He was grinning as he came out of the small washroom. In fact, he was so distracted that he walked straight into another body.

'Oh, excuse me,' said the body, flustered, and dropped a washbag.

Steven dived for it chivalrously. The body was a tall woman with an untidy bush of hair and a tired face. As he handed the bag back to her he thought that she looked as if she had not closed her eyes since they left New York.

'My fault,' he said compassionately. 'Sorry about that.'

She shook her head, hugging the bag to her breast. 'Don't be. I shouldn't be up here anyway.'

The aroma of coffee had been joined by the smell of hot rolls. Passengers in the first-class cabin were still resting peacefully, but presumably other people were being shaken awake. A continental breakfast was clearly imminent some-where. He made the obvious deduction.

'Do I take it you're an invader from economy class?'

'Yes.' She eyed him warily.

Steven was impatient. Did she think he would call an at-tendant and complain? So much for his piratical appearance! It obviously took more than a missed shave to make him look like a free spirit.

He said ruefully, 'Good luck.'

He realised that he was blocking her path. He began to move aside with a word of apology—and the plane banked.

Two things happened simultaneously. The jet-enhanced sunrise lit the cabin with gold. And the woman staggered. Her eyes flared, as if she had suddenly been recalled to her-self, but it was too late. There was nothing to hold on to. She tipped forward, dangerously off balance, and began to tumble.

Steven caught her. Well, of course he caught her. He was a gentleman. And anyway, that was what he was good at, thought Steven wryly. It was what he was designed for, with his rugby player's build and his judo-honed muscles. Strong and stable. He was not charming, and he had never been handsome, but by golly he had always been good at stopping women falling on the floor.

So good that he almost managed to repress the leap of the senses that hit him fair and square.

For in the blazing dawn she was suddenly amazing—no longer a tired woman with tangled hair. She was a golden-skinned goddess with a wild red mane. More than red—flame and scarlet and crimson and bronze, flickering like living fire. As it brushed his mouth it smelled of leaves. In his bracing arms her body felt unbelievably soft… Steven swallowed.

Ouch! One rejection of the morning razor, one lurch of a plane, and he was into seriously politically incorrect territory.

Hold on, there, Steven Konig. You're not Captain Blood and never have been.

He restored her to her feet fast.

'I'm so sorry,' said the goddess, flustered.

She did not seem to have noticed his reaction.

'My pleasure,' said Steven. He could have kicked himself the moment he said it. It sounded as if he had been hanging around just waiting to get his hands on her.

But the goddess did not seem to be on political correctness patrol just now, thank God. In fact the goddess was looking adorably remorseful.

'Did I hurt you?' The soft voice had an accent he did not recognise, and Steven was good at accents.

'Of course not.'

Steven was charmed that she should ask, though. It was a long time since anyone had asked if they'd hurt him. The brilliant and influential Steven Konig was not supposed to have any vulnerabilities at all.

But his golden Venus was still worried about him.

'That was so clumsy of me. I just wasn't concentrating.'

'I was standing in your way. Don't worry about it.'

She gave him a shy, grateful smile. His flame-haired Venus was *shy*?

'No, it was my fault. I had stuff on my mind. Sorry.'

'I know the feeling.' And for some reason he found himself telling her a truth, suddenly. 'I end up taking stock of my life when I'm on a plane. Coming down can be a shock. Brace yourself for landing; here comes your life again!'

She laughed. She had exactly the right sort of laugh for a goddess. It was a warm gurgle, as warm as that amazing hair and full of delighted surprise. Steven felt as if he had been given a prize.

'You are so right,' she said with feeling.

He beamed at her. Flustered and rumpled and honest, she was the sweetest thing he had seen in a long time. He had a sudden urge not to let her go.

'Is this your first time in England?'

And at once thought, How stupid; that accent could even be English.

She was shaking her head but she did not crunch him. 'No.

But I haven't been here for years. I'm going to have to do the Tower of London and St Paul's Cathedral all over again. If I have time.'

'Time? It's really a business trip, then?'

'You could say that.' She had a dimple at the corner of her mouth when she wanted to smile and was trying to repress it. Steven stared, fascinated. All goddesses should have dimples, he decided. Made them more human. More approachable.

He said on impulse, 'If you're doing the sights, you should certainly take a trip out to Oxford. The old colleges are pure fairytale.'

She let herself laugh aloud then, and the dimple disappeared. He would have objected but her dancing eyes made up for it.

'That's a great marketing job you're doing. Has the town got you on a retainer?'

'City,' he said automatically. 'No, but I live there.' He smiled into those warm brown eyes. It was a heady feeling. 'The place is a jewel. You ought to see it if you haven't.'

She shook her head. 'No. Well, not that I remember.'

He was intrigued. 'Amnesia?'

'I wish.' This time the dimple flickered only for a moment. She gave a sharp sigh. 'I was born in England, but my mother died when I was five and my father took me to Peru.'

He was fascinated. 'And you've never been back?'

'Well, not seriously. Once with the school for a few days, a long time ago. But it wasn't easy—' She stopped. Then said explosively, 'Hell, why cover it up any more? There was a family feud. The Other Side lived in England.'

He pursed his lips in a soundless whistle. 'Big stuff. I didn't know people still had family feuds. Not having a family myself, I suppose I wouldn't.'

The dimple reappeared. 'Congratulations.'

He laughed aloud, enchanted. 'So, this trip is of the nature of a peace summit?'

She jumped. 'Not really. Though I've thought about it,'

she admitted cautiously. 'But I'd have to do a lot of tracking down. I don't know where to start.'

The goddess had a chin that Napoleon would have been wary of—and a voluptuous, vulnerable mouth.

Distracted, Steven said, 'I bet you'll find a way. I bet you could do just about anything you set your mind to.'

She gave him a smile like sudden sunshine. 'That's what I've always been told.'

'Well, then—?'

She laughed. 'They may not want to see me,' she pointed out. 'People have been brooding on this feud for a long time.'

He found his mouth widening into his wickedest grin. 'Montagues and Capulets,' he said. 'They'll be fascinated. Trust me.'

She was doubtful. 'Do you think so?'

'Positive. What's more, it makes you much more than a tourist. So you must definitely come to Oxford.' He felt in his pocket for a business card. 'It's your heritage. You're coming home.'

'*Home!*' She flinched as if he had kicked her. The wonderful smile died as abruptly as if someone had flung a switch. 'I don't think so.'

A man, thought Steven at once. It had to be. In his experience, a woman only flinched like that at the word 'home' if there was a man involved. Was she fleeing an unhappy relationship? Or was there a man she wanted who wouldn't make a home with her? For some reason Steven hated the idea of that.

He stuffed his business card back and took his hand out of his pocket.

Or maybe the man wanted her to move in with him. Anyway, her reaction to the word 'home' had nothing to do with a load of long-lost relatives. Oh, yes, it was a man all right.

He stopped his thoughts right there. Either way, it made no difference to him, did it? He was not the sort of man to pick up women in mid-air. And his shy golden goddess did not look like the sort of woman to let herself be picked up anywhere.

Nice idea, Steven. Not practical. You're not Captain Blood and you haven't got a pirate ship to carry her off to. Get yourself a shave and a tie and get back to normal!

He stepped back and gave her one of his public smiles—courteous, regretful, remote as the moon. He was invulnerable Steven Konig again.

'Well, have a good one, whatever you decide to do. Safe landing!'

'Th-thank you.'

Or he thought that was what she said. He did not wait to hear her reply.

See that fantasy; let it go. He said it to himself savagely as he made his way back to his seat. He was thirty-nine years old and far too many people depended on him to keep his head. Fantasising about goddesses was for teenagers.

CHAPTER TWO

PEPPER brushed her teeth and did what she could to get her tangled hair back into order. She must have looked like a complete zombie. The man had stared at her so hard. Then again, poor guy, she had nearly knocked him over. It wasn't surprising he'd stared. He would have the bruises to show for the impact tomorrow, she thought, wincing.

Oh, well done, Pepper! Your first encounter with someone who won't connect you with the Calhoun millions and you do your best to cripple him!

At least he had not looked at her as if she was a potato.

But he hadn't asked her for a date either.

Pepper shook her head at her image in the tiny restroom mirror. So what? Who ever heard of someone asking a woman for a date in the middle of a plane? Especially when she had literally bumped into him only two minutes before. But there was a moment when she had almost thought he might. There had been something—

Her eyes flared, remembering that moment when his hands had closed round her. Surely it wasn't just her imagination? She had hardly been able to see his face, the dawn light had been so strong in her eyes. But she'd sensed that his expression had become intent, as if he had suddenly touched live power. She had noticed because it was the exact same thing she had felt herself. Raw energy. Magnetic attraction. *Sex.*

Her mouth dried, thinking about it. She was not used to feeling uncontrollable sexual attraction to complete strangers. She gave herself a brisk mental shake.

Okay, *you* may have had an adolescent moment, Pepper. But, let's face it, you're not at your best right now. That's no reason for him to start lusting back at you.

Concentrate on the evidence. You walked into him and he was *nice* about it. He didn't yell and he didn't threaten to sue. Isn't that enough to start with?

It was. It had to be. Anyway, it was the first hopeful thing that had happened for weeks. Give thanks for a civilised Englishman's good manners and don't ask for the moon, Pepper told herself practically.

Still, she made her way back to her seat with a smile on her face. And when the chatty passenger in the next seat started a conversation again, she even replied.

The woman was a grandmother from Montana who had never been to London before. In fact, she confided, she had never flown long distance before. She refused Pepper's invitation to change seats, but she did crane across her to look out at the landscape below as the plane came in to land.

'It's big, isn't it?' She sounded awed.

The flight was early. Very early. The sun was barely up as they came in to land at London Heathrow. It glittered on buildings and planes. To Pepper, leaning her forehead against the bulkhead, even the runway looked as if it was studded with diamonds. On the ground nothing moved.

In the cabin, there was that air of suppressed excitement that came from being woken too early, fed croissants and orange juice you didn't want, and throttling down from five hundred miles an hour. And being about to step out into a new country.

Or, in Pepper's case, a new universe.

Maybe the Englishman was right. Maybe she should try looking for her cousins. How hard could it be? And she was going to have plenty of time.

Grandma Montana swallowed. Suddenly, after all the hours of chat, she blurted out the cause. She was going to meet her unknown English son-in-law and her two English grandchildren for the first time. She was real nervous, she confessed.

Pepper did not know what to say. 'That's a new concept for me. My grandmother has never been nervous in her life.'

'She must be very brave.'

Pepper was crisp. 'If people never cross you, there isn't that much to get nervous about,' she said tartly.

It felt good to say it. She sat straighter in her seat.

The airbus hit the runway and there was a loud rushing noise of giant brakes. Grandma Montana gave a little gasp. She was very pale.

To her own surprise—well, she was Mary Ellen Calhoun's granddaughter, and, until a week ago, designated heir to Calhoun Carter; she didn't *do* emotion—Pepper took the older woman's hand.

'Everything's fine. It always makes a noise like that.'

Grandma Montana's smile wavered. 'Thank you. I was sure it was really. But—' She gave Pepper's hand a squeeze, as if Pepper were her own family and entitled to that intimate little gesture. 'I'm being silly. You're very kind.'

It hit Pepper like a ten-ton truck. Kindness! Outside Calhoun Carter, people were kind to each other without expecting a return. The man she'd knocked into had been kind about it. Now this woman was thanking her for a gesture that her grandmother would have laughed at.

She nearly said, No, I'm not. I've never been kind in my life. There's no room for kindness in business. And I'm a business woman to my toenails. I've got three degrees and my own biography at *Fortune* to prove it.

Nearly.

Only somehow she didn't. Somehow she thought— But I don't have to stay like that. I can change. The unshaven man with the sexual force field around him had said she could do anything she set her mind to. And she could. She *could*.

So she said slowly, 'You're not silly. Doing anything for the first time is scary.'

'I suppose so.' The woman sounded doubtful.

The brakes were off and the airbus had come out of its wild thrash down the runway to a stately prowl. She let go of Pepper's hand. For a moment Pepper nearly took it back again.

She said abruptly, 'Are your family meeting you?'

'I sure hope so. But they might not have got here yet. We're so early.'

'Tail wind across the Atlantic. Happens a lot. They'll probably allow for it.'

Pepper's companion began to look more hopeful. 'Do you think so?'

'People do,' said Pepper, who had been met by chauffeurs all her life. Astonishing herself, she said, 'Look, would you like me to stay with you until your daughter gets here?'

The woman looked as if she had won a lottery. '*Would* you?'

'Sure. No problem.'

'But you must have people meeting you—'

'No,' said Pepper steadily. 'Nobody meeting me.' *Ever again.* 'I'll be glad to stay with you. Really.'

But in the airport her good intentions hit a setback. A voice behind her called, 'Ms Calhoun? Ms Calhoun?'

She turned instinctively. It was a financial journalist for an international press agency. She knew him slightly.

'I thought it was you,' he congratulated himself. 'I was sitting behind you.'

Oh, one of the partying entrepreneurs. He wouldn't have believed his eyes, seeing her travelling outside business class. Pepper bit her lip. Having avoided the financial pages so far, she really didn't want to be caught out in London.

But he seemed unsuspicious enough. 'What are you doing here? Are Calhoun's thinking of taking over a British company?'

After only a momentary pause, she held out her hand.

'Not a business trip,' she said firmly. 'How are you, Mr Franks?'

His eyes were shrewd. 'Just back from New York. I've been covering the sustainable trade talks. What are you doing in London?'

Pepper remembered her conversation with the unshaven pirate. 'I've got family here,' she said, inspired.

He was sceptical. 'Really?'

'Really.' She took rapid stock and told him part of the truth. 'I haven't had a holiday in quite a while. I'm told London in spring is beautiful.'

He pursed his lips, clearly unconvinced. But handling inquisitive journalists was all part of a day's work for Pepper. She gave him a bland smile. He gave up.

'Have a good time. If you could do with some company any time, give me a call.'

He fished a business card out of his wallet and handed it over. She managed not to wince. There had been a moment when she'd thought the pirate was going to give her *his* card. Now that would have been a triumph indeed. A man who didn't know she was an heiress giving her his number!

'Thank you,' said Pepper, not looking at it. She thought wryly, Now, this is much more the sort of pick-up I'm used to.

The journalist was offering a classic bargain—dinner, or a night on the town, maybe a bit of inside information, in return for an exclusive on Calhoun Carter's next move on the acquisition trail. He wouldn't have bothered to say a word to Pepper if he had known that Mary Ellen had kicked her out.

The luggage carousel began to turn. She gave him a nod of farewell.

'Excuse me. I'm going to be walking someone who's new to London through Customs. Goodbye, Mr Franks. Nice to see you.'

But she kept his card. In the survival game you held onto any advantage you could get, however unlikely.

Steven looked for the glorious redhead in the baggage arrivals hall. There were so many people that it would have been a miracle if he'd found her. But he still looked.

Other people kept getting in the way, though. Martin Tammery, a pushy alumnus of Queen Margaret's, returned to the attack, trying to persuade him to come on some new television game show he was starting. And he and Sandy Franks kept arguing about someone they'd seen in the crowd. The Tiger Cub, they called her.

Uninterested, Steven barely heard them. He wanted a goddess, not a tiger cub. He scanned the surge of people. Surely that fiery mane could not disappear so easily?

Martin Tammery took on an acquisitive expression. 'Do you think she'll be here for long? Could I get her on to *In My Experience*?'

Sandy Franks pursed his lips. 'You'd have to move fast. She never stays anywhere long.'

'Yeah. But if she's here on some secret deal the London office will deny all knowledge. How do I get hold of her?'

Sandy's eyes gleamed. 'Ask me along to the recording and I might just help you out. I have contacts.'

'There you are, Steven. That's the class of company you'd be in if you come on the new programme,' Martin said to him. 'What about if I do a deal with you, too? If I get Pepper Calhoun on the programme, you stop wriggling.'

'I have no idea who Pepper Calhoun is,' said Steven, not taking his eyes off the crowd.

They both started to give him a potted biography. He paid no attention. There was a gleam of red on the other side of the luggage carousel. He started after it.

In vain, of course. By the time he got there the crowd had parted and closed up again too many times. She was lost, his golden Venus with her shy smile and her infectious laugh. And that mouth that brought him out in a cold sweat just to think about.

He should have asked for her number right then, when he'd had the chance, and to hell with political correctness. He should have given her his card. At least then he would have *known*.

The other two came panting up after him.

'So what about it, Steven?' said Martin. 'Do the pilot show? For the honour of the old college?'

Steven sighed deeply. But, as the newly appointed Master, he had obligations to old alumni.

Here was the real world kicking in again, he thought wearily. Goodbye, dream of a goddess. Hello, duty.

'Send me a proposal,' he said quietly. 'I'll have to check the diary. But in principle I'll do anything I can.'

Martin Tammery was exuberant in his thanks. 'Great. I'll count on that.'

He could, too, Steven thought, as he trailed his suitcase out into the main concourse and agreed to share a cab back into central London with the other two. Steven never let people down.

Story of my life, he thought with a touch of bitterness. Steven Konig, the ultimate sustainable resource. Always there for Queen Margaret's College. For Kplant. Chairing a conference here, delivering a lecture there. Never rebelling. And never, ever giving in to impulse.

Which is exactly why I'm travelling in to London with two men who want more lectures and interviews and wise words, he thought with irony. Whereas what *I* want is my golden goddess here alone with me.

What would have happened if I had given her my card? Would she have given me her number? Agreed to meet? Maybe even been here now?

He went hot at the thought.

And where would we have gone from there?

Just the question filled him with wild longing. It was so acute that he winced. His companions, deep in conversation about employment law, did not notice.

Just as well, thought Steven, crushing the picture that his reflections had brought to leaping life. He was still influential Steven Konig with all those responsibilities. He still had no spare capacity to run a private life as well.

But he wished he had. He could not remember ever wishing anything so much. If only…

The other two broke off their conversation.

'What was that, Steven?' said Martin Tammery blankly.

Steven's smile was full of self-mockery. 'I just said Captain Blood had all the fun.'

*   *   *

Pepper found that life as a non-rich person was surprisingly easy. In lots of ways, it was even fun. And the best thing of all was not having to think how her grandmother would react to everything she wanted to do.

She had never stayed anywhere but five-star hotels before, all pre-booked by efficient Carmen. So it was an adventure to find herself a modest hotel to stay in.

It was a relief that she came through that all right. She even managed to negotiate with the concierge when he said that she had to wait until midday to take possession.

'I've had a bad time. I need to sleep for a week,' she said, yawning hugely. She brought out her remaining credit card. 'I'll pay for last night, too, if you want. Just lead me somewhere I can lie down.'

Either the yawn worked or the concierge was someone else with an unexpected streak of human kindness. Within ten minutes she was stretched out on a hard bed, her eyelids closing.

'First problem solved,' she said to herself drowsily. 'So shucks to Mary Ellen Calhoun.'

She did not wake until the evening. And even then she just got up and had a slightly dazed walk through dark streets before falling back into bed.

The next morning she felt entirely different. Not hopeful, exactly. More interested. The pirate on the plane had said she could do anything she put her mind to. So—was he right?

After a good night's sleep she was ready to find out. She had even half formulated a plan. She went out and got herself a mobile phone and began putting it into practice.

Problem solving seemed to be her forte. By the end of the day an old contact had agreed to look at her business plan for *Out of the Attic*. Another had offered to make some introductions. She'd found a temporary job to get her through the next few weeks. It was only word processing, but at least it meant that she did not have to dig into her small store of capital—or spend hours on her own thinking about the vicious little darts that her grandmother had thrown.

She'd also made a decision that surprised her. She had the name of a lawyer who had acted for her mother's family years ago. She went back through the files on her laptop and there it was, a reply to a letter he had sent her on her twenty-fifth birthday.

'Tell them you want nothing to do with them,' Mary Ellen had said.

And Pepper had. So she'd been shamefaced in approaching him today. But that piratical endorsement had got her through the first hesitation. She'd called the lawyer.

He had been cool, but he had not refused to see her.

'This is a surprise,' he said when she came in. 'Mrs Calhoun always insisted that you did not want to see anyone from the Dare family.'

'That was then.'

He looked sceptical.

'I've been disinherited,' she told him baldly.

'Ah.' He pursed his lips. 'So what exactly do you want from the Dare family?'

Pepper flushed. 'Not money, if that's what you think,' she said indignantly. Being thought a sponger was a new experience she could have done without. 'I can look after myself. But—I just thought—if anyone in my mother's family wanted to see me, I'm going to be in London for a while. We might get a cup of coffee some day. That's all.'

'I see.' The lawyer pondered.

She said with difficulty, 'I don't remember my mother, you see. Since—I mean, recently I've been thinking about that. And I think I'd like to meet my aunt. This feud thing has gone on too long. I don't even know what it was about.'

For the first time the lawyer smiled. 'I'll ask,' he promised.

He must have asked swiftly. Now, at the end of the day, Pepper was taking a phone call in her hotel room.

'Pepper?' said a voice that bubbled over with enthusiasm. 'Oh, I can't believe this. It is so good to talk to you after all these years.'

'Who is this—?' began Pepper, and then fell over her own words.

She knew that voice. She still had dreams of it saying, 'Come on, what does it matter if you get dirty? You're going to see the kingfishers.'

'Isabel?' she said in disbelief.

She had thought it was a dream. Her grandmother had said it was a dream. Or a prolonged case of a preschooler's imaginary friends. Mary Ellen had even threatened to take her to a psychiatrist—'To get it out of your system for good and all.'

'*Izzy?* Izzy, is that you?'

Izzy's laugh had not changed either. In the memory that Mary Ellen had said was disturbed fantasy, she and Pepper had visited together just once when they were children. Izzy must have been about eight—and muddy; Pepper had been ten, in her best dress—and longing to be muddy, too.

Now Izzy sounded just the same as she had in Pepper's memory: as if she could take on the world—and have the time of her life doing it.

'Yup. It's me,' said Isabel Dare ungrammatically. 'I gather you're over in the UK for a while. Want to come and play?'

Pepper sat down hard in the overcrowded little room. In the mirror on the opposite wall, she saw that she was grinning all over her face. She embraced the disputed memory with relish. More, with laughter.

'You've got more ditches for me to wade through?'

'You remember, then?' Izzy gave a choke of amusement. 'Better than that. I've got a spare room that just happens to be empty. Fancy sharing a flat with your cousins?'

And Pepper thought, *Home!*

She had never shared with friends of her own age. It was a revelation.

Pepper had never come out of her room at the Calhoun mansion until every hair was neatly in place. Isabel and

Jemima thought nothing of wandering around in their underwear with their hair in curlers while they swapped plans for
the day. They shared clothes and housework and invitations
with careless freedom. Then fought to the death over a low-
fat yoghurt. They read each other's horoscope aloud over
Sunday breakfast. They split bills without arguing but battled
over whose turn it was to wash up a couple of coffee cups.
After a week of stunned disbelief, Pepper began to talk, too.

At first it was just little ironic asides. 'I've lived in New
York, Paris and Milan. But I've never lived in chaos before.'

'Good experience for you, then,' said Izzy cheerfully.

But Jemima was curious. 'You must have. I mean you
were a student, right? Everyone lives in chaos when they're
a student.'

'Not me. I had my electronic personal organiser. And a
maid.'

'A *maid*?' they chorused.

'Well, someone to do the housework.'

'We do our own housework,' said Jemima firmly.

'Unless Jay Jay is giving a party for all her cool friends,'
said the irrepressible Izzy. 'Then we call in a stylist to run
it. And a firm of industrial cleaners afterwards.'

Jemima threw a cushion at her.

There was some truth in the accusation, though, as Pepper
found out. Izzy's friends were a casual bunch, but Jemima
took her socialising seriously.

'It's because she's a fashion model,' Izzy told Pepper
when they were alone. She sounded unwontedly serious. 'She
seems to make a decent living. But her agent says she could
be really big. That's what the networking is all about.'

'I know about networking,' agreed Pepper with feeling.
'I've been trying to put together a new retail idea. The busi-
ness plan is beautiful. Now all I have to do is get the capital.
Networking rules!'

That was when she moved on to full-scale confidences.
Well, she didn't tell them everything. Not 'you're a potato'

and 'I paid men to date you'. But why she left Calhouns. And what she was trying to do in London.

'And if it all collapses, I can hire out as a consultant,' she ended flippantly. 'That's what unsuccessful entrepreneurs do between projects.'

'So tell us about *Out of the Attic*,' said Jemima, a dedicated shopper.

Pepper lit up. She loved her project.

'It does two things. Most important, it looks at shopping as a form of entertainment. It has to be comfortable, stimulating, and aesthetically pleasant. So we turn a shop into a treasure trove. You don't go through racks, you discover things. As if you were going through an attic, in fact.'

Jemima, the clothes professional, pursed her lips. 'But you want people to move through the shop fast, buying as much as they can carry?'

'They can buy. The stock is on site. But clients have the chance to look at things in a pretty environment before they decide what they want to try. They check their coats and bags at the door. They can get a coffee. They can sit and look at stuff.'

Jemima was unconvinced. 'Sounds like an awful lot of effort to sell one garment.'

'It would be. But most people will buy more than one. And they'll take a catalogue home with them. We're talking lifestyle here. And building a customer base.' Pepper was warming to her theme. 'I'm thinking we should have a Girls' Night Out facility. An exclusive show for a few friends after work.'

Izzy was enthusiastic. 'Great. Shopping and a party at the same time.'

Pepper nodded. 'That's what I thought.'

'But you don't shop and you hate parties,' Jemima pointed out.

'So? There aren't enough people like me to build a business on. I know what other people want.'

Jemima stayed sceptical. 'And what would the clothes be like?'

'Well, it wouldn't just be clothes. They're too seasonal and subject to fashion.'

'You mean you don't know,' Jemima crowed.

Pepper was stung. 'I know. I've got a couple of designers on standby. The brief I gave them was pretty and practical.'

Jemima looked down her nose.

'You probably don't want to believe it,' Pepper told her with feeling, 'but most clothes in the mall are designed for adolescents who don't feel the cold, never sit down and think they ought to be sexual predators. There's this great big market out there who don't fulfil the brief. My clothes will be for them.'

'You mean the Size Fourteen Syndrome,' sniffed Jemima.

Pepper glared. 'And what is wrong with being size fourteen? Do you know how many people are?'

Jemima opened her mouth, caught Pepper's eye and thought better of it.

'There's only one problem with being size fourteen,' Pepper announced. 'It's not cool. I'm going to make *Out of the Attic* so cool no one who comes in will be ashamed of herself, no matter what size she is.'

Jemima cast her eyes to heaven. 'Dream on.'

But Pepper was unmoved. 'I've done the market research. And I've lived size fourteen. Women are just waiting for *Out of the Attic*. You'll see.'

'Excuse me, Master.'

Steven was miles away. He was standing by the high window staring down into the quad.

Not with pleasure. Other people saw a medieval hall the colour of warm butter, with mullioned windows that overlooked a succulent velvet lawn. Steven saw crumbling stonework, blocked guttering and the cost of a new roof that made his eyes spin just to think about.

Queen Margaret's College was an ancient institution and a historic building. It was also broke.

Valerie Holmes, who had been the Master's secretary for so long that she remembered when Steven Konig was a new undergraduate, looked at him with sympathy. Poor chap, she thought. He was the classic compromise candidate: neither the pure academic that the old guard wanted, nor the racy media darling that the politicians had been pushing so hard. As a result, he was disliked by both sides. And he knew it.

She coughed gently. 'Master?'

Steven jumped and turned guiltily. 'Oh, it's you, Valerie,' he said, surprised. 'Is the car here already?'

He had an appointment to do a television interview and they were sending a car for him. It was Valerie who had insisted on that. She knew how much he hated the publicity stuff. But when you were Master of a college that was falling down you had to do it.

But this was not the car reluctantly provided by Indigo Television. This was something a lot more troubling. Though Valerie was much too discreet to say so.

'No, Master. The car won't be here for another hour.'

Steven sighed. He pushed a hand through his dark hair. She really should have reminded him to have it cut, thought Valerie, momentarily distracted. But at least he had shaved this morning. Sometimes, when he strode in from his morning jog round the Parks, he looked more like a guerrilla who had been in the jungle for too long than a senior member of the university.

He gave her his best grin, the conspiratorial one that made his eyes twinkle. Not a lot of people saw that grin. Most of them thought the Master of Queen Margaret's College was a dour workaholic. And those were his supporters. Valerie knew different—as she told her husband.

Now he said, 'So what is it, Val? Do you think I need a pep talk?'

'Of course not. It's—'

'Don't worry, I've read my briefing. Very thorough, as always.'

'Thank you. The stuff from Indigo Television was a bit thin. But—'

'You tell it like it is, don't you, Val? This one is going be grim,' said Steven.

He went back to the big eighteenth-century desk that he habitually covered with papers, letters, reports and old sandwich packing. He began to rootle among the debris. He had only been in the office two hours and the silt was already several layers deep. Valerie sighed and retrieved an empty paper cup and several engraved invitations. She tossed the cup into the wastepaper basket and shuffled the invitations absently into date order.

'It's not the programme—' she began.

But Steven had found her careful notes.

'"*Reaching for the Moon,*"' he read aloud. '"*Good ideas and bad business.* Discussion chaired by Gordon Ramsden—"' he looked up briefly '—who sounds a pillock from your notes—and American retail consultant Penelope Anne Calhoun—who sounds worse.'

'Master—'

'"Daughter of the Calhoun dynasty".' He was reading aloud. '"Main board member of Calhoun Retail and associate Vice President of Calhoun Carter, the parent company, until she left to attend business school aged twenty-three. Still only twenty-eight and a sought-after speaker".' He looked up. 'Yeah, right. What the hell is she going to know about trying to get a new idea off the ground? Or struggling to raise capital? She's had capital on a plate. And I bet she's never had a new idea in her life.'

Valerie said loudly, 'Steven, there's a woman at the porter's lodge who says you're the father of her child.'

Steven stopped clicking his tongue over the attributes of Penelope Anne Calhoun and looked up, his eyes suddenly blank.

Val said more gently, 'The porter says she insists on seeing you. He's tried, but she won't go away.'

Steven still said nothing.

Her voice rose. 'Steven, there are undergraduates down there. People are in and out of the porter's lodge all the time. Think of the *scandal*!'

He flinched visibly.

'I mean, I'm sorry Master,' said Valerie, reverting to formality now she had his attention.

He did not say anything for a moment. But the wicked schoolboy look disappeared completely. Suddenly he was completely without expression.

At last he said, 'I assume she has a name, this woman?'

'Courtney. She wouldn't say any more.'

'Ah.'

'I told the porter that your diary was full. That you had an engagement in London. That she had to call and make an appointment. He says—she just won't leave.'

'No,' he agreed, still expressionless. 'She wouldn't.'

So he *did* know her! So maybe the rest was true, too?

Somehow, Valerie didn't think so. Steven Konig was not an easy man to know, but she would have staked her life that he would not walk out on his own child.

He said, 'How long have I got before I have to go and listen to Penelope Anne Calhoun's thoughts on why inventors make bad businessmen?'

Valerie gave a little spurt of startled laughter. Steven Konig was an inventor and a businessman and was rapidly building a reputation for being brilliant at both.

'Well?'

'The car will be here at eleven.'

He nodded, his mouth hard. 'Fine. I made some notes. Statistics and stuff.' He flung a diskette at her. 'They're on that. Print them off for me, will you? I'll go down to the lodge and collect Mrs Underwood.'

'Mrs—oh.'

'Her name,' he said deliberately, 'is Courtney Underwood. She was married to Tom. You may remember him. Big guy, mountaineer, read chemistry. He was killed in the Andes four years ago.'

'Of course,' said Valerie, wooden.

'I am the child's godfather,' he said, taking pity on her. 'I haven't seen her or her mother for years. Neither Tom nor Courtney were big on keeping in touch.'

'I *see*.'

'Relieved?' he said sardonically.

Valerie puffed. 'Nothing to do with me,' she said haughtily. But, yes, secretly she *was* relieved. In secret. The college could do without a scandal on top of its crumbling finances. And Steven didn't deserve it, so hard as he was working.

He gave her a faint shadow of that sweet smile. 'You lie in your teeth, Val. But never mind. I forgive you. I'll get rid of her. And then it's off to the studios in glamorous Wandsworth to sing for the college's supper. Just don't forget to print those notes out for me.'

Then he was out of the office, running down the stone staircase as lithely as ever he had when he was an undergraduate.

Valerie went out onto the landing and called after him. 'Master—what's the file name for your notes?'

He did not pause. But he looked up, head back, eyes gleaming with wicked laughter. Goodness, he's sexy when he's off his guard, thought Valerie.

'Balderdash.'

And he disappeared out of the front door, into the rainy spring morning.

Valerie bit back a laugh and went to tell the porter that the Master was coming down to deal with the importunate visitor. And then to print off his file. And to wonder if the widowed Mrs Courtney Underwood thought he was sexy, too.

* * *

The widowed Mrs Courtney Underwood was still as beautiful as ever. Steven saw it at once. He halted in the doorway of the porter's lodge, unobserved for the moment.

Courtney was talking animatedly to the porter. She looked exactly the same as she had the morning she had told him she was going to marry Tom, thought Steven. Soft dark hair that shone like wet tar, voluptuous mouth pouting sweetly, prettily apologetic—and quite, quite immovable. The porter was looking harassed.

Steven sympathised. He knew the way Courtney had of making you feel helpless. And the porter had done nothing to deserve it.

Unlike me, thought Steven, wincing inwardly. Unlike me.

He stepped forward. 'All right, Mr Jackson. I'll deal with this.'

Courtney swung round, quick as a snake.

Just like old times, thought Steven, managing not to wince. Courtney liked being in control. She didn't like anything—or anyone—to surprise her.

Then she caught herself. 'Steven! Darling!'

A couple of undergraduates, going through the pigeonholes for their mail, stared unashamedly at the Master and the glamorous new arrival.

Courtney flung herself into his unwilling arms, ignoring her audience. No, thought Steven wryly, make that *relishing* her audience. While all the time she pretended to ignore them. Oh, yes, same old Courtney.

Save me from women who play to the gallery, he thought. Out of nowhere he remembered his golden Venus, flustered and shy, and divinely unaware of her sexiness. For some reason, it gave him strength.

'Hello, Courtney,' he said, at his most dispassionate.

'"Hello, Courtney",' she mimicked, leaning back and looking up into his eyes reproachfully. 'Is that all I get? After all this time?'

As if to illustrate her point, she ran her hands up under the dark grey jacket of his suit. He felt the warmth of her fingertips burn through the crisp cotton of his shirt like sun through a magnifying glass.

Oh, yes, she was just the same all right. Still with that camellia skin and long, long lashes. Still with that trick of letting her eyes fill up with tears so that they sparkled like diamonds but did not actually fall and make her eyes red. And her lips slightly parted for a kiss.

Steven did not kiss her.

There was a time when those brimming, sparkling eyes had twisted his gut into knots. And she had known it. Beauty was licensed to do any damn thing it liked in Courtney's world. When she'd run off to India with rich, reckless Tom, he'd thought he would never recover.

But that was fifteen years ago. Surely even Courtney, who was brilliant at not seeing things she didn't want to, would realise that Steven Konig was out of her thrall by now.

And I am, Steven told himself fiercely. I am.

He detached her hands and stepped away from her. 'You'd better come to my room.'

She gave a little wriggle.

'Sounds like fun.'

He kept his face blank, though he was annoyed with himself.

'Don't get excited. It's only an office.'

He led the way out into the windy outer quad. Students milled round them. Their scarves whipped about in the breeze as they balanced books and bicycles.

'How clearly I remember all this,' said Courtney, looking around.

For a moment Steven was so angry he could hardly speak. 'You surprise me.'

She stared, momentarily disconcerted. 'What do you mean?'

He took a moment to master himself. 'As far as I remember you only came to Maggie's once,' he said curtly. 'The Commem Ball. You remember that? When you picked up Tom?'

'Steven!' She seemed genuinely shocked. 'Surely you're not still bitter about that? Not after all these years.' Shocked, sure. But quite pleased, too.

Steven could have kicked himself.

He said in his most deadpan voice, 'Just setting the record straight.'

She laughed. He'd used to think that girlish laugh so charming. Now it set his teeth on edge.

'Oh, Steven! Still fussing over details.'

'Facts are important,' he said.

Her brows twitched together in irritation. For a second she did not look so charming. That was new, he thought. Of course, he had never argued with her in the old days.

He said levelly, 'You were never in and out of college. In fact, you hated my being at college at all. I remember some scathing comments about dating a student. So let's not re-write history.' He led the way through a small brick arch. 'This way.'

He could feel Courtney watching him. She said softly, 'You are so wrong. I don't have to rewrite a thing. I remember—everything.'

The breathy little word was for his ears only, like a private caress. He remembered that trick, too. It was shocking how quickly the old helpless rage boiled up.

He set his teeth. He was thirty-nine years old. He had not responded to Courtney's needling in fifteen years.

'I'm glad to hear it.'

She caught his arm, bringing him to halt in the lee of the old wall. He looked down at her. Her eyes were wide.

'I remember that ball,' she murmured, watching his mouth. 'So clearly. Didn't we kiss right here?' She took a step closer.

She had changed her perfume. This one was cloying and over-spiced, like an opium den. For a moment Steven's head swam. He drew a ragged breath.

Courtney smiled. 'See? I *do* remember.'

Oh, she remembered her devilish game all right. Every time he'd seen her again she had pulled him back onto his knees, with some caressing remark, some implicit promised intimacy that he did not want to want but somehow could not quite put out of his mind. Eventually he had given up seeing Tom entirely. It had felt as if he was skirting betrayal all the time. In the end it was easier just to keep away.

'Convinced?' said Courtney, all charm and sweet, unstated challenge.

Steven stepped away.

'We never kissed in this archway,' he said crisply. 'It only leads to the Master's Lodging. Twenty years ago I never came through here. It was out of bounds.'

He turned away in disgust. No doubt she would get out of the hole she had dug herself. Courtney was good at that. He just didn't want to watch.

He unlocked the ornamental gate and led the way into the Master's house. It was the oldest part of the college, a late medieval tower, with a spiral stone staircase and some fearsome gargoyles. Normally Steven smiled at them as he passed. Now he did not even look at them.

He put his head round the door of the secretary's room.

'Mrs Underwood is joining me in my study for a few moments, Valerie. Could we have coffee, please? And let me know when the car arrives.'

He opened the door to his study and stood back to let Courtney precede him. The new perfume was powerful stuff. It was stifling.

He closed the door behind her and then strode across the room to fling open a window.

'So—have a seat,' he said, keeping as much furniture between them as he could manage. 'This is a surprise. What are you doing in Oxford?'

She was not stupid. She knew that he had deliberately retired behind the magnificent oak desk. She let her eyes fill.

'Don't be mean to me, Steven.'

And she still had that little catch in her voice, he thought, irritated. From nineteen to twenty-four it had set his pulses racing. Now he was thirty-nine and had exactly forty-eight minutes before he had to leave for an interview. And that little squeak was *still* sexy.

After all this time! How could he be such a fool? He stopped playing nice.

'What do you want, Courtney?'

She blinked those wonderful lashes. Fifteen years ago it would have brought him out in a cold sweat. But in the intervening period he had known a lot of women. These days he recognised it for what it was—a charming little trick that she turned on and off at will. Oh, for his flustered goddess who had no tricks! The thought startled him with its intensity.

Courtney did not notice that she had lost her audience. 'Oh, Steven,' she sighed. 'Are you still hurting after all these years?'

He looked at his watch. 'Whatever this is about, Courtney, I suggest that you shift it along,' he said courteously. 'I've got an appointment in London and a car coming at any moment.'

She moistened her lips, still watching him intently. He remembered that trick, too. In spite of himself, he felt his body respond. *Damn.*

She saw his expression. 'Send the car away,' she said huskily.

He stared at her, unblinking. 'You really think that you can get anything you want, don't you, Courtney?'

She widened those wonderful blue eyes. 'You were always too clever for me, Steven.'

Oh, he was clever, all right, thought Steven with savage self-mockery. Three degrees and more research papers than you could shake a stick at. And the once eager lover in him still went weak at the knees when she looked at him like that. Even though he knew it was all a sham. Even though his instincts reminded him of red hair and a shy laugh that was no sham at all. *Idiot!*

'I think that depends on how you define clever,' he said, full of wry self-mockery. 'Come on, Courtney, I haven't got time for games. What is it this time? Money?'

A faint look of annoyance creased the creamy brow. She sighed.

'You've got so—so commercial. I hardly recognise you.'

'It's a tough old world. I'm surprised you haven't found that out, with a child to look after.'

She bent her head. Her dark hair shone. The uneven Victorian glass in his leaded windows fractured the thin spring sunshine into a hundred rainbows. It made her look as if she were surrounded by a halo. Did she know that? thought Steven, irritated.

But he was relieved, too. He found it easiest to resist Courtney when she was in her ineffable Madonna mood.

'Actually, that's why I'm here. I need to talk to you about Windflower,' said Courtney, at her most soulful.

His eyes narrowed. 'Yes?'

When Tom died, Courtney had arrived at the Underwood household claiming to be penniless. Steven had been in Australia at the time. He'd got back to find Tom's widowed mother on the verge of bankruptcy. She had also been watching over the baby every night while Courtney went out to ultra-smart restaurants with men she said goodbye to in their darkened-windowed limousines.

'Courtney's a bloodsucker,' Mrs Underwood had said, clear-sighted but despairing. 'I'd kick her out, but Windflower is my grandchild, poor baby. You're the only one of Tom's friends I can talk to. You're the child's godfather, for heaven's sake. I need help, Steven.'

So Steven had helped. After Courtney took off again— with one of her shady escorts—it had not been easy. But over the years he had set up schools, holidays, medical programmes and once even an emergency flight out of a war zone.

Mrs Underwood told him he was a saint. Steven himself had the uneasy feeling that he was throwing money at a problem when he ought to be doing something a bit more hands-on.

Now he said, 'What about Windflower?'

Courtney put her haloed head on one side and looked winsome. He wanted to slap her.

'I need to leave her with you.'

He was so totally braced for a request for money that for a moment he did not register what she was saying.

'What?'

She repeated it.

'But—' He could not get his head round it. 'What on earth are you talking about?'

'I'm going to a healing centre. Adults only. I can't take her with me.'

Steven was even more taken aback. 'A healing centre? What's wrong with you?'

Again there was a flutter of annoyance. 'Spiritual healing,' said Courtney, with something of a snap.

Steven was momentarily speechless.

She tossed her head, defiant. 'My counsellor says I need calm.'

He found his voice. 'Are you serious?'

'My inner child needs nurturing.'

'Oh?' said Steven awfully. 'And what does your outer child need? Your real child, I mean. The poor little soul you've dragged around over half Europe for the last several years.'

'If you think I'm such a bad parent, you try it,' flashed Courtney, suddenly a lot less ineffable. 'Fine godfather you are. When did you last spend time with her?'

'When was she last in the country?' he retorted.

'You could have had her to stay with you. But, oh, no. That would get in the way of your glamorous bachelor lifestyle,' said Courtney resentfully.

Steven drummed his fingers on the desk. 'You were the one who told me a child needed to stay with her mother,' he reminded her. 'Rosemary Underwood would have loved to adopt her.'

Her eyes narrowed. 'I'm not talking about adoption. I'm

talking about time out,' she said flatly. 'Windflower needs to build a relationship with a father figure. You. Now.'

It was just the same as it always had been. Why hadn't he remembered that arguing never worked with Courtney? She was too armoured in her own self-will. Common sense didn't stand a chance.

Even so, he said reasonably, 'But I don't know anything about children.'

Courtney shrugged. 'Then employ a nanny. You can afford it. Or take a course. Marry. Whatever.' She flung her hands up in the air. 'It's your turn for a bit.'

'My *turn*!'

The telephone on his desk rang. He picked it up. 'What?' he said curtly.

'Sorry, Master. Didn't mean to interrupt.' It was Valerie. She sounded shaken. 'Jackson's on the phone. He says is it all right if he takes the child to the buttery for a bun?'

Steven froze. 'Child?' he said with dangerous quietness.

Courtney was looking out of the window, unconcerned.

'Apparently a little girl has come into the porter's lodge. She says she's with Mrs Underwood.'

Steven saw red. 'You mean my visitor dumped her nine-year-old daughter somewhere in Oxford.'

'Er—'

Courtney looked round.

'Leave it with me.' Steven put the phone down. He said with deadly quiet, 'You brought the child with you, then?'

'Of course.' She was surprised. 'I haven't got anyone to leave her with.'

'And left her precisely where?'

Courtney shifted her shoulders pettishly. 'Outside in the street. I told her I'd only be a moment—'

'A *moment*?'

Yet only minutes ago she had been telling him to send the car away and... How long did she think it would take her to seduce him, for God's sake? Steven's anger flamed so hot that he could barely see.

'Why on earth didn't you bring her in with you?'

But he knew why, didn't he? Courtney had wanted the nine-year-old out of the way while she batted her eyelashes at susceptible Steven Konig. *Stupid* Steven Konig, with his low flashpoint and his old-fashioned chivalry.

He came out from behind the oak desk. No need to stay in the bunker now. He was so angry he could barely remember that he had ever desired her.

'We are going to get her,' he said grimly.

'You go. It's wet out there—'

'*Now*, Courtney.'

Rational argument might not work. But sheer rage did, apparently. She came without a word, though as soon as they were outside she shivered ostentatiously in her fashionable scarlet coat. Steven refused to notice.

At the porter's lodge, Steven skirted ten battered bicycles and steamed into the warmly lit room. It had filled up. A couple of undergraduates were having a cheerful argument with Jackson, and a girl staggered under the weight of a parcel she was retrieving from about the old wooden pigeon-holes. Almost invisible among the damp jeans and armfuls of books, a small girl was standing in front of the untidy noticeboard. She was attentively reading a flyer for a Hallowe'en party in the junior common room.

Steven stopped dead.

The small girl turned round. In contrast to her mother's, her clothes were not only unfashionable, they looked inadequate. It was warm enough in the porter's lodge, but her pale face was pinched with cold. She was clutching the sort of pack he was vaguely aware of seeing children wear on their backs to school. Her fingers were blue.

She gave him a long level look. He thought, *Tom*.

There was a click of stiletto heels behind him. 'There you are, Windflower,' said Courtney, putting her arm through Steven's. 'You remember your godfather?'

'Hello,' said the small girl, neutral.

'Hello,' said Steven.

'He's going to take care of you for a bit,' said Courtney firmly.

Steven ignored her. He hunkered down in front of Windflower. 'Do you know who I am, Windflower? Really?'

'One of Mummy's old boyfriends?' said Windflower dispassionately. But she swallowed as if she was scared.

Steven curbed his fury. This was not the child's fault.

'Do you *want* to stay with me?'

Windflower's expression was a study in amazement. 'Mummy says I'm going to.'

Clearly she didn't often get asked her opinion. Steven's heart twisted.

He stood up. 'I'll need her papers,' he said, icily practical all of a sudden. 'Birth certificate, medical records, school attendance.'

'Windflower's got all that in her school bag,' said Courtney, demonstrating more planning than he would have expected.

'And her things?'

She waved a hand at a battered suitcase under the noticeboard. It was not, thought Steven, very big to hold all the child's worldly possessions.

He took one of his famed lightning decisions.

'Right. You want me to look after her.' He was in the grip of a cold fury the like of which he could not remember. 'I'll look after her. Jackson, I need your keyboard.'

His voice was very quiet and courteous, but Jackson nearly fell over the furniture to open the door of his little office to admit him. The undergraduates stopped joshing, startled.

Steven got into the word processing program and typed a page very fast. While it was printing, he swung round.

'You two,' he said to the two young men, 'I shall want you as witnesses.' He flung two sheets of paper at Courtney. 'There you are. You assign the care of your daughter to me absolutely. You put your forwarding address there—' His forefinger stabbed the paper so hard it nearly broke it. 'And you *sign.*'

She quailed. 'But I don't have an address.'

'Then write down that you have no address.' Steven was still quiet. Still reasonable. And quite deadly. 'On both sheets. And sign at the bottom.'

She did. At last she looked shaken. He brought a dark fountain pen out of his breast pocket and did the same. His signature was a great dark slash, like a dagger-tear in fabric.

'Witness,' he said to the undergraduates. 'Name, address, date. Both pages.'

Soberly, they did what they were told.

Jackson came back. 'The car from Indigo Television has arrived, Master.'

'Find him a parking place and tell him I'll be ten minutes,' said Steven, still icy.

He flung one of the signed copies at Courtney as if he could not bear to touch her. Then he folded the other carefully and put it in his inside pocket with his pen.

'Look after the suitcase for me, will you, Jackson. I'll pick it up later.'

He held out his hand to the child. 'Would you like to come to a television studio? See the cameras?'

She thought about it. Nodded.

'Then say goodbye to your mother and come with me.'

'Goodbye—?' Courtney was startled. She made another grab for his arm. 'But we have so much to talk about...'

'My solicitor will be in touch,' said Steven, unmoved. He removed his arm. 'I told you I had an appointment.' And, to the small girl, 'Say goodbye. I've got to hurry.'

Windflower kissed her mother in a subdued way and then slipped her hand into Steven's. He had been quite right. Her fingers were freezing.

He sent Courtney a look of such icy contempt that she took a step back. He did not kiss her. Or wish her goodbye. He did not say anything else at all.

Instead he said to Windflower, 'In the car, you can tell me about yourself and what you'd like to do. Come with me while I get my stuff. Jackson, see Mrs Underwood out of college, would you?'

'Certainly, Master.'

Without another look at Courtney, Steven led the child inside the college walls.

Behind him, he heard Jackson say, 'Would you like me to call you a taxi, madam?'

God bless phlegmatic college servants, he thought. Of course they were used to dealing with brilliant eccentrics. Jackson would take this drama in his stride.

Now all Steven had to do was take a crash course in the habits and nurture of nine-year-old girls.

But first he had a television lecture to deliver.

'You know what I really hate about the British?' said Pepper Calhoun broodingly.

She glared at her reflection in the mirror. Terry Woods bit back a smile. Terry was British. She had been doing Pepper's hair for two months now and she knew her client's occasional tempers very well. It usually meant she was winding herself up to do something she didn't want to.

'No, Pepper,' she said cheerfully. 'Tell me. What do you really hate about the British?'

'They're so damned good at blackmail.'

'Blackmail!' Terry was so startled she nearly dropped her scissors. 'Sorry about that,' she said, recovering. 'Didn't scratch you, did I? Have a chocolate to calm your nerves!'

Pepper glowered at her in the mirror. 'That's what I mean. Blackmail.'

Terry was bewildered. 'Sorry?'

'You fumble your scissors, I'm gonna yell. Got a right to yell. Got a real good yell building, just waiting to be let out. Then you go and spoil it all by offering me chocolate. Blackmail!'

Terry laughed aloud. 'That's not blackmail; that's insurance.' She leaned over Pepper's shoulder and pushed the lit-

tle dish of chocolate hazelnuts along the counter towards her.
'Help yourself.'

Pepper hesitated. 'I shouldn't.'

Terry combed the thick wet hair carefully. 'So, who else
is blackmailing you? Izzy?'

Izzy never went near a hairdresser, but she and Terry met
in the newspaper shop in the morning before work. It was
Izzy who had sent Pepper along in the first place, having told
her cousin crisply that she could not afford uptown salons
any more and offered her a brisk recommendation to sample
Battersea's best.

'Not Izzy. Indigo Television,' said Pepper, even more
gloomy.

'Never heard of them.'

'Why doesn't that surprise me?'

'So who are they?'

Pepper shrugged. 'Some bunch who managed to track me
down. And I'm being nice to financial journalists this month.
So...'

She narrowed her eyes at her reflection as Terry began to
wind brightly coloured worm casts into the damp tresses.
Pepper's hair was thick and naturally curly, but today she
had announced that she wanted the full pre-Raphaelite mane.

'I'll need more than that.'

'Even more curls?' Terry had said, startled.

'As many as you can squeeze out of that tube.'

'Why?'

'Because I've got to look cool and happening. And sweet.
And a good investment. All at the same time.'

Terry gagged. 'I'm a hairdresser, not a magician.'

'Think babe-with-a-heart. That'll do it.' Pepper bared her
teeth in a terrifying smile.

Terry quailed. 'Right you are. Heart it is,' she said dubi-
ously.

She combed and twisted and flicked with speed. But she
was still intrigued.

'What's this in aid of? Whojimaflip TV?'

'Indigo Television,' announced Pepper, 'is the reason I'm in here at ten o'clock in the morning, sure. I have to do babe-with-a-heart for someone else. Venture capitalists, the bastards! Superior, British, male venture capitalists. But at least they won't be scared out of their wits by a crazy grandmother.'

Venture capitalists bored Terry, and she didn't understand the bitter reference to crazy grandmothers. 'What are you doing on telly?'

'Good question,' said Pepper, depressed.

Her fingers strayed towards the chocolate hazelnuts. She hauled them back and clamped the hand in her lap.

'A studio debate.'

'Oh.'

'I ought to be sitting with an ice pack on my head, thinking up the marketing line of the century,' she said bitterly. 'I've got just five hours to come up with it. And I'm fresh out of ideas. So what am I doing? Messing about on Indigent Television talking to a bunch of students. Huh!'

Terry waved aside the missing marketing line of the century. 'Great. When can I see it?'

'If you watch lunchtime television.' Pepper's tone was not encouraging.

'Ace. There's a telly in the back. When?'

'Today. It's live. I must have been out of my mind.'

Terry whistled. 'Coo. What's it about?'

'How to be an entrepreneur.' Pepper fished around in the bag propped against the leg of the salon's black and silver chair. She brought out a scrubby piece of paper. '"*In My Experience,*"' she read aloud. '"This is an educational programme in a new format. Each week we will be inviting two up-and-coming figures from the world of commerce and technology to take questions from an audience of young people about to start their careers." Sexy—not.'

Terry could not deny it. 'Never mind,' she said comfortingly. 'It's all publicity.'

'That's what I keep telling myself. In between intervals of beating my head against the wall.'

Terry stuck in the last pin and stepped back, eyeing the sci-fi confection in the mirror knowledgeably.

'It can't be that bad.'

'You've missed the three salient facts,' said Pepper. 'No advance warning of the questions. No fee for appearing. And no audience figures.'

'Oh.'

'I could well be making a total idiot of myself in front of the producer's grandma and his dog walker.'

'Then why do it?'

'That blackmail word. God, I hate the British.'

Terry found an errant strand of hair. Swiftly she unwhirled one of the worm casts and stuck the hairpin in her mouth. 'Which blackmail word is that?' she asked through clenched teeth.

'Education,' snapped Pepper. 'If you're in business in Britain, you're supposed to do *anything* for education. Unpaid.'

For the first time in her life she was living on a tight budget. It was, as she told Terry, a useful experience. But it did not increase her charitable tendencies.

'So why are you doing it?'

'Good PR. At the moment I need all the publicity I can get.'

Terry stopped primping her client's hair and stared at her in the mirror. This was a subject on which she had heard Pepper, the daughter of one of the richest families in America, twenty times or more in the last two months.

'But I thought you hated publicity.'

'I do,' said Pepper, her mouth drying at the thought. 'But I need it. Or my project does.'

Her stomach rolled in sympathy. It was too much. She could not resist any longer.

She reached for her first chocolate hazelnut of the day.

*   *   *

Steven finished reading Indigo's briefing and pushed the papers into his briefcase. Beside him, Windflower was as composed as if she travelled in limousines every day of her life. Her feet didn't touch the floor, though.

Conscience stirred. Steven said gruffly, 'This may be a bit boring, I'm afraid.'

Windflower—poor child; how on earth did she cope with a name like that?—turned wise eyes on him.

'It's all right. I'm not a nuisance. Mummy says I'm not.' She did not sound boastful. She sounded resigned.

Conscience stopped stirring, got up and kicked him on the shins.

'As soon as this blasted programme is over you can be as much nuisance as you like,' Steven said with fervour. 'I promise.'

But at that moment the car turned into what looked like a junkyard. Steven knew that Indigo Television was young and struggling. He had not expected uniformed flunkeys and an atrium. But even he was surprised by the black bags of garbage and an old fireplace leaning drunkenly against the wall of a corrugated iron shed.

He leaned forward to the uniformed driver.

'Are you sure this is the right place?'

'That's what they all say,' said the driver with gloomy satisfaction. He eased the limousine into the tiniest possible space in the lee of the corrugated iron wall and cut the engine. 'Back at two, right? Unless you want to stay on for the hospitality.' It sounded as if he did not expect it.

What sort of hospitality went with corrugated iron? Illegal moonshine and pork scratchings? Steven's lips twitched in spite of himself.

'Two o'clock will be fine.'

The driver got out and opened the door with a flourish. Windflower scrambled out, then shivered in the cold air.

'We must get you some warm clothes,' said Steven, following her.

A woman was coming through the yard as carefully as

Courtney had picked her way round the bicycles. Steven had the brief impression of a bundle of wet mackintosh and a voluminous headscarf before the woman accosted him.

'Hey, is this dump for real?'

It was so much what he thought himself that he grinned.

'Afraid so. Do I deduce that you're another guest of Indigo Television?'

'Guest?' She snorted. 'Victim, more like. What do they do to make you feel welcome? *Not* mug you?'

The driver said, 'This way sir, madam.'

The door was narrow, but it gave onto a corridor that at least was pleasantly painted in pale colours, with pictures on the walls and some sophisticated concealed lighting.

The lady in the mackintosh layers was not impressed. She stepped inside out of the wet but did not go down the corridor. Instead she raised her voice.

'Hey! Junkyard TV! Anybody home?'

Behind her, Windflower giggled. Steven looked down at her in surprise. It was the first time he had heard the child laugh, he realised.

There was no reply. The lady in the mackintoshes sucked her teeth, considering. Then suddenly she stood on one leg and whipped off her shoe. And began to pound rhythmically on a convenient radiator.

The noise was indescribable. Steven winced. Windflower hopped in sympathy and began to join in. A steel band in a subway would have been a whisper by comparison.

'Enough,' said Steven.

Windflower stopped. But her evil genius went on, banging and hollering. The shoe with which she was hitting the radiator, Steven saw, was black patent leather, high-heeled and expensive, with a pirate buckle. So underneath the swathes of mackintosh there was another chic woman used to getting whatever she wanted.

Steven decided that he didn't have half as much sympathy with her as he'd thought he did.

'I'll deal with this,' he said.

He stalked down the corridor, throwing doors open as he went. At the third, he was successful.

'You have guests,' he told the two startled girls chatting in front of the ladies' room mirror. 'And hearing loss, apparently. Move.'

They scurried out into the corridor. Mackintosh woman stopped pounding the ironwork when they appeared. But she eyed them with the look of one about to start again at the slightest provocation.

'Give her a coffee, a seat and somewhere to leave her coat,' Steven advised them.

The girls rushed to comply—one in the direction of the coffee machine, the other urging the small party through one of the anonymous doors with unintelligible half-sentences of apology. Windflower skipped along happily. But mackintosh woman hung back.

She looked at him broodingly. 'Do people always do what you tell them to do?'

'Always,' said Steven with composure. 'You'd better put your shoe on. Need a hand?'

In the act of pushing her foot into its constricting pump, she stopped dead, arrested. Under the monster headscarf—was she wearing curlers under there?—her face was startled—and furious.

He gave her his sudden, wicked, blinding smile. 'Always,' he said again. 'You see, I'm always right.'

CHAPTER THREE

ALWAYS right?

Pepper could not believe he'd said that. Nobody ever said that, even if they thought it. Even if they were superior, British and male.

Even if they were a superior British male who was built like a boxer and magicked television receptionists out of mid-air.

She lowered her foot to the floor. 'What planet did you stop ruling to be here?' she flashed.

At least it got rid of the smile. That I'm-the-Lord-of-the-Universe and Aren't-you-lucky-I'm-so-charming smile. For a moment he looked absolutely blank. *Good!*

He held out his hand. 'Steven Konig. Here for *In My Experience*.'

'I must be here on the wrong day, then.'

It confused him. 'What? Why?'

'I'm here to do a programme on entrepreneurs,' she told him innocently. 'Not tyrants.'

'*Tyrants?* Because I told you to put your shoe on?'

Steven Konig, whoever he might turn out to be, shook his head. He stopped being taken aback and decided to be amused. Pepper could have danced with rage.

'Isn't that overreaction?'

Pepper *hated* being laughed at. She felt the tension in her jaw. 'You tell me. You're the one who's always right.'

'Er—' said the girl Steven had routed out from the rest-room to act as guide. She was hopping on the spot. 'Would you like to come this way? We do have a hospitality room.'

Pepper's eyes flamed at her. 'And Lord Zog here told you

to give me coffee, too, didn't he? Sure. Let's do what the High Command commands.'

The girl gave her a scared smile. 'I know Martin is anxious to meet you,' she said unconvincingly. 'This way…'

The hospitality room turned out to be an airless, windowless room with basic chairs round the wall and a corner table full of used plastic cups. Steven Konig, whom Pepper was rapidly coming to loathe, raised his eyebrows.

The girl gathered up the dirty cups rapidly. 'Er—can I take your coat?' She looked at Pepper's bundled figure. 'Coats?'

But she went to stand behind Steven Konig, to receive his immaculately tailored grey coat. Pepper, it seemed, could shift for herself.

In spite of her simmering rage, Pepper told herself not to be petty. It was not the girl's fault that she leaped to do the bidding of Lord Zog. She'd bet just about everyone in the world did.

He unloaded his coat, with a charming smile that clearly did not see the girl at all, and brought out his cellphone. Soon he had planted himself in the corner, where the reception seemed to be best, and was talking on it rapidly. And ignoring everyone else.

Huh! No surprise there, then!

Pepper put down her briefcase and shrugged out of her top layer. It was a serviceable hooded waterproof cape that Terry, professional that she was, had insisted on lending her. 'You've got to keep your hair dry,' Terry had said firmly. 'Put it on top of your mac if you're cold. But I haven't spent hours on all those curls for you to go and let the rain ruin them.' So now Pepper felt like a bag lady as she unpeeled her inelegant coverings.

There was a sound, somewhere round her hip. Pepper looked down, startled. Lord Zog's small girl looked back unwinkingly.

It made Pepper uneasy. She didn't know anything about small girls.

The small girl pursed her lips. 'Why are you wearing two coats?'

It was a reasonable question. Even knowing nothing about children, Pepper could take reasonable questions in her stride.

'Because my coat doesn't have a hood and the cape does.'

The small girl digested this. 'But you've got a scarf. Why do you need a hood as well?'

'Because the scarf isn't waterproof and I've just had my hair done,' said Pepper literally. She undid the knotted silk and drew the large scarf off her head with care, shaking out the red-gold mass.

On his telephone, Lord Zog made a strangled sound. It sounded as if whoever he was talking to had just given him the shock of his life. *Good*, thought Pepper.

The small girl was not interested in her accompanying adult. Instead she transferred her gaze from Pepper's face to the tumble of hair, now gleaming with Terry's model-girl conditioner. Her expression stayed neutral.

'Cor,' said the girl with the dirty coffee cups, momentarily distracted. 'Your hair is *gorgeous*.'

Pepper was taken aback. 'Thank you.' She almost said, I'll tell my cousin. Then decided that it didn't sound cool enough.

She looked round, but there was no mirror on the wall. Pepper put up a hand, blind. Miraculously, it seemed as if the pre-Raphaelite curls were still curling and bouncing. They responded to her Hair Alert Test—that was, they sprang back when tugged gently. Now all she had to do was make sure that the top had not been too flattened by the headscarf and she was ready to face the cameras.

'Where did you find that colour?'

Pepper stared. 'What?'

'I've always wanted to be a redhead. But whenever I try it ends up looking like a fire engine. Who does your colour?'

'My parents.'

'It's *natural*?' Disbelief.

'Been a redhead all my life.' Pepper was torn between

amusement and embarrassment at the admiration. She fluffed up her hair, more self-conscious than she wanted to admit.

The girl sucked her teeth. 'You weren't—er—expecting make-up or anything, were you?' She looked covertly at Lord Zog, talking on his mobile telephone again, with his back to the room. 'Indigo hasn't been going very long. We haven't got all the trimmings yet.'

Pepper frowned. There was a message here, if she could only work it out. 'So?'

The girl shuffled under her burden. 'You might want to go to the ladies'. Um—touch up your make-up,' she volunteered reluctantly. 'TV lights—you know.'

'Your nose is shiny,' the small girl interpreted dispassionately.

Pepper curbed a strong inclination to swear. She hardly ever used make-up and today there had seemed no point; it would only have washed off. Terry's shampooing technique was thorough and enthusiastic, but you came out of it looking like an Olympic swimmer. A trip in a chilly taxi, followed by a sprint through the rainswept obstacle course that was Indigo Television's forecourt, would not have modified that. Of course her nose was shiny! Why on earth had that not occurred to her before?

'Thank you,' she said to the small girl. And to the other, 'Where?'

'I'll show you.'

The small girl hooked her hand firmly into Pepper's. Pepper jumped. She could not remember holding hands with a child before. Come to that, she could not remember holding hands with *anybody*.

The small girl, however, seemed to find holding hands with a perfect stranger perfectly normal. 'Me, too,' she said firmly.

Lord Zog looked up from his telephone conversation. Whatever it was, it seemed as if it had shaken him. He looked stunned.

Not stunned enough to be civil, though. 'Where are you going?' he said sharply.

The small girl sent him a look of mingled contempt and warning. 'I want to *go*.'

He frowned irritably. 'Go where?' And then he clocked what the warning was about. 'Oh. Go. Yes, of course. Will you be all right with Ms Er…?'

Never mind whether Ms Er was all right with this unlooked for responsibility, thought Pepper, raging inwardly.

'Thank you,' she said coldly, 'we'll be fine.'

She stuffed her briefcase under her arm and stalked out before he could reply. To her surprise, the small girl trotted beside her as if Pepper was a fully trained childminder.

'Down here,' said their guide. 'It's a bit dark, but…'

She flicked a switch and a line of lights bright enough to guide down a jumbo jet came on round the biggest mirror Pepper had ever seen. In their pitiless glare she looked too pale, too windswept and—yes, scared. Damn!

'You've got twenty minutes or so before we do the warm-up,' said the girl helpfully. 'But we'll be running tight after that. It goes out live, you know.'

'Yes,' said Pepper, trying to ignore the butterflies that had taken up residence under her ribcage. 'I know.'

'That's all right, then. See you back at the hospitality room.'

She went, leaving her two guests alone. Pepper looked at the child warily. But the small girl took herself composedly off to one of the cubicles without asking for assistance.

Pepper heaved a sigh of relief. This whole thing was proving hard enough without having to turn herself into a mom out of a cake mix advert. She swallowed.

You can do this, she told herself silently. You can do whatever you have to.

She emerged from her own cubicle to find the small girl inspecting the hand-drier and a purple perfume dispenser.

'Mummy,' she announced, 'says you should always wear

the same scent. So when people smell it they think about you.'

'Does she, indeed?' said Pepper, who could not tell one scent from another. Mrs Lord Zog sounded a prize pain in the ass. 'How original.' She glared at herself in the mirror.

Sharing a flat with her cousins had proved an education. Jemima was a highly paid model. She was hardly ever there, but only last week she had herded Pepper and Izzy into her bedroom and imparted a serious lesson on make-up.

London had given Pepper a number of shocks. One of the biggest was that aspiring entrepreneurs had to look the part. As the favoured granddaughter of a retail dynasty she had never had to worry about how she looked before. She dressed in a dark business suit, kept her hair tidy and wore good, plain jewellery in gold or platinum. That was enough, or so she had always thought.

Not any more. Potential investors looked at her business plan, her graphs and her product description and said, 'Hmm, yes, maybe.' And then they sat back and waited for her to charm them.

'I don't know anything about charm,' she had wailed at her cousins, beginning to panic.

That was when Jemima had launched into her crash course.

So Pepper, a professional to her fingertips, had grimly mastered the art of twenty-first-century face painting. Now her armoury contained a complete kit of powders and colours and soft pencils, together with a couple of brushes. If she concentrated hard she could even remember what to do with them. She squared her shoulders and pulled the pack out of the briefcase.

The small girl hauled herself up onto a stool beside Pepper and inspected the collection.

'Mummy,' she announced, considering and discarding a smoky lilac eyeshadow, 'says colours are for the evening.'

'Thank you for your advice,' said Pepper, not meaning it. She took the lilac eye shadow up defiantly and leaned forward, peering.

Her eyes were really her best feature, she thought. Unless you liked hair the colour of red squirrels, that was. But her eyes were velvety brown, slightly tilted, with the longest lashes in the world. She brushed a little lilac shadow onto one eyelid and inspected the result.

The small girl said nothing.

Pepper sighed and fished out a make-up removal pad. 'Okay, I'll give you that. It looks like I've been through ten rounds with an Olympic heavyweight.' She scrubbed it off. 'It will just have to be powder, then. Maybe a bit of blusher.'

She brushed on porcelain face powder and surveyed herself critically. Well, it certainly took the wind-and-rain shine out of her face. Maybe it made her look just a little ghostly? But the last few weeks had taught her caution with blusher. It was all too easy to end up looking like Mrs Punch. She flicked the tiniest dusting of colour over her cheekbones and stood back.

Maybe still too pale? Well, it would have to do. They had not asked her onto the programme for her glamour-girl looks, after all. She bit back a wry laugh at the thought. And at least her nose wasn't shining any more.

She flicked a comb through her hair, lifting the front where it had been flattened a bit by the headscarf. Pursed her lips. Gave up.

'That will have to do.'

The small girl said, 'Aren't you going to spray your hair?'

'No,' said Pepper, revolted.

'Mummy—'

Pepper was beginning to loathe the sound of the word.

'I'm sure she does, but I haven't got time,' she said crisply. 'Come along.'

Once again the child tucked her hand into Pepper's uninvited. In spite of herself Pepper softened. Well, a bit. It wasn't the child's fault that Pepper was feeling jumpy and out of her depth.

As they went along the corridor she tried to put herself in the child's place. If she had been told that she was going to a television studio she would have expected a great treat. This airless bunker must be a real disappointment. Pepper could remember disappointments like that.

She said with suddenly real sympathy, 'Have you been looking forward to this for ages?'

The child shook her head. 'Uncle Steven said I had to come. Afterwards,' she explained, 'we are going shopping.'

'Uncle! So Lord Zog—I mean, Mr Konig isn't your daddy?'

The small girl shook her head.

'What's your name?'

'Janice,' said the child, so quickly that Pepper blinked.

She might not know much about children, but Pepper had been dealing with plausible businessmen all her life. She could smell an untruth a mile off. She knew, as sure as eggs was eggs, that the child's name was not Janice. Interesting.

Steven had cut the call the moment she walked out of the room. He snapped his cellphone shut. Then sat down rather hard.

It was *her*! His golden goddess! That hair was unmistakable. Though its riotous tumble was clearly no longer due to a hard night courtesy of David Guber's airline but several hours in some upmarket hair salon.

But—her hair was not the only thing that was different. All these weeks he had been cherishing a private memory of fleeting tenderness. He had let himself dwell on it in snatched moments of quiet. Had found his lips curving into a smile, as if he were looking into her eyes, whenever he was alone for too long.

Well, so much for tenderness! This woman was not the elusive creature of his dreams. This was a multi-mackintoshed harridan who banged radiators with her shoe and went to war as soon as look at you. She might not be sweetly manipulative like Courtney—she was *worse*.

Steven ground his teeth. Oh, boy, what a great judge of

women he had turned out to be! Fifteen years on and he was still making the same mistakes! Had he learned *nothing*?

The door banged back on its hinges and the producer swept in.

'Hi, Steven. Sorry I wasn't around when you got here. You know what it's like! Met everyone?' He was scribbling on his clipboard.

'Not exactly,' said Steven with restraint.

'Yes, I heard you'd already had a run-in with the Tiger Cub.'

'I take it you mean Ms Calhoun?'

'Yup.' Martin Tammery looked up briefly. 'Isn't she something?'

'Indeed,' said Steven, as frostily as any of his Victorian predecessors as Master of Queen Margaret's. 'Though, to be fair, I cannot state positively that it was Ms Calhoun. She did not do me the courtesy of introducing herself.'

Martin stopped scribbling. His eyebrows rose. 'Whew.'

'I assume, however, that is who the woman was. On the basis of Indigo's briefing.'

'Er—yeah.' A grin began to break through. 'Looks like it's going to be a lively programme. Great. Where is she? Or have you savaged her so badly she won't even stay in the same room?'

'Very funny,' snapped Steven. 'That woman is more likely to beat me about the head with a stiletto heel.'

Which was the exact moment at which she came back into the room with Windflower.

'Ms Calhoun,' said Martin with enthusiasm, surging forward.

She had done something to her face, thought Steven. Her eyes looked larger—even larger—and deceptively melting. Deceptive! That was the word to hang onto.

'Don't think you and Professor Konig have been properly introduced,' said Martin wickedly. 'Let me do the honours. Steven's a big name these days. But he was my tutor when I was at college. Steven—Ms Pepper Calhoun.'

Pepper was taken aback. Behind the producer, Lord Zog was glaring like a hanging judge. There were not a lot of ways to play this one, short of eyeball to eyeball. And that might not be a good thing before they went on television together. Pepper passed her options under rapid review and decided on breezy good humour.

'Hi, Professor.'

She held out a hand. Being British, male and superior he would have to shake it. She had come to know the type. They might be cold as ice and hard as reinforced concrete, but they made a fetish of good manners.

Professor Lord Zog ground his teeth visibly. But she had read him right. He took her hand and shook it firmly.

Pepper bit back a smile. 'Big name, huh?' she said innocently. 'Sorry I don't recognise you. I've only been in the UK a couple of months.'

'I know,' said Lord Zog arctically.

Pepper bit back a smile. 'Tell me what I should know about you,' she invited.

But that didn't annoy him as much as it ought to. For a moment he looked fixedly at her mouth, his face absolutely expressionless. And then he began to look faintly amused.

'Martin exaggerates. I'm a simple biochemist, Ms Calhoun. I got my invitation to the ball because I set up a company called Kplant which has had a bit of luck.'

Bit of luck? Pepper was taken aback. Kplant had been the success story of the new companies sector three years ago.

She frowned. 'Food technology, right? On the edge of getting a full quote?'

For a moment he looked taken aback, then said smoothly, 'You're a little premature. Maybe. In the fullness of the time.'

Pepper's eyes narrowed. She thought, He's said that before. And he's wary of me. Why?

Aloud she said, '*Maybe?* But surely every guy wants his business to turn into a quoted company? That's the point of starting a business in the first place.'

His expression didn't change. But somehow she knew she had hit home. She thought, I've made him mad.

'You think so, do you?' There was an odd note in his voice.

Pepper thought, No, I haven't made him mad. Actually, that's given him a real kick. That's exactly what he expected me to say. And he despises me for it.

Their eyes locked. Smouldering.

And Pepper thought—*Hey, I know this guy.*

Martin intervened. 'Hey, guys. Save it for the programme. In fact, let's go to the studio now.' He flipped a hand at one of the hovering girls. 'Take care of Ms Calhoun's little girl for a bit, will you?'

'She's not—' said Pepper.

But he was already off, talking hard. He shot them along the corridor, running rapidly through the details of the format, the signals they would get. 'The audience are sixteen to eighteen. Wide achievement range. Lively, from what we've seen so far. Interested in everything from the music business to banking. You may get some unexpected questions. Can you handle them?'

Steven Konig shrugged. 'I'll play it by ear.'

And what about me? raged Pepper silently. Or does he think he's going to be doing all the talking? Yeah, I just bet he does. I asked him about his damned company but he hasn't asked a thing about me. He doesn't think I count at all!

But still she couldn't get it out of her mind that she had met him somehow, somewhere before. But *where*? And if she remembered why didn't he?

Except, of course, that he probably hadn't thought she counted last time either. She gritted her teeth and marched into the studio behind him, telling herself to keep calm. She needed to present an image of a woman in control. It wasn't going to help her cause if she started off by kicking Professor Steven Konig on live television. But it was a temptation. Pepper had to admit to herself that it was a temptation.

Later, she promised herself. And pinned on a professional smile as she took her seat and looked round at the cameras.

Steven could feel her bristling at his shoulder. His lip curled. What had she got to bristle about? He was the one who had been wasting his time for weeks—no, make that months—daydreaming about a completely fictional woman!

Time to wake up, he told himself grimly. No, time to *grow* up. He listened to the host's smooth introduction and simmered.

The first question went to Pepper. It was from a girl in tattered jeans asking about start-up capital. Pepper answered sensibly enough. For some reason that made Steven's irritation bubble over.

'You would, of course, know so much about raising capital,' he said, almost before she had finished. 'With the huge resources of the Calhoun empire behind you.'

The host blinked. Before he could intervene, though, Pepper was sitting bolt upright in her chair and glaring.

Steven frowned so mightily that his strongly marked brows nearly met.

'Face it,' he said implacably. 'You have a load of advantages that the rest of us can't call on. Family money, family business, tradition, contacts—'

To say nothing of a good line in make-believe innocence! Good enough, in fact, to sucker in even a man who'd thought he knew every damned trick that women were up to. Oh, no, Pepper Calhoun had no right to bristle.

'You've got it made,' he concluded. A muscle worked in his jaw.

Pepper gave him a glittering smile. How could he ever have been attracted to the woman? He must have been lightheaded with tiredness on that damned flight.

'An entrepreneur has to use everything he can,' she said sweetly. She smiled round the audience. 'You will all have people you know. They will have skills or contacts. Use them. The British seem to think it's not fair, somehow. You have to grow out of that.'

Steven stiffened. She's calling me a schoolboy, he thought in disbelief.

Their eyes met. She smiled again. That smile said, as clearly as any look could, Round One to me, I think.

It set the tone for the rest of the programme.

'Oh, *yes*,' muttered Martin Tammery in the control box, swinging between the monitors. He hugged himself in ecstasy.

The audience picked up the edgy atmosphere. Soon they were asking questions aimed at bringing either Pepper or Steven out of their corner fighting.

It was all within the bounds of civilised behaviour—just. But there was no disguising the fact that the two distinguished guests loathed each other. And then, suddenly, it went out of control.

And the question which started it could not have been more innocent.

'So do you think it's fair that women should be asked to lose weight in order to get a job in a boutique?' someone asked.

Steven looked bored. He drummed his nails on the arm of his chair.

Pepper fielded it smoothly. 'Yes, I've read about that case. I think it reasonable for an employer to expect an employee to take care of his appearance. And if we're realistic we tend to choose staff to reflect our client base, for all sorts of good marketing reasons. But weight as such is a different issue. There are all sorts of reasons why people become overweight, and some of them they can't help...'

And all of a sudden Steven's simmering anger exploded.

'Oh, please. That is such nonsense.' He slewed round in his chair and glared at her. 'It's a simple equation. If you take in more energy than you use in exercise you store up fat. You can do something about it or you can ignore it. But don't give me that nonsense not being able to help it. If it was important enough you would do something about it. And

I'm tired of women banging on about their weight as if it's nothing to do with them.'

He was thinking of Courtney as he said it, with her thousands of excuses for doing exactly what she wanted and her complete refusal to accept responsibility for anything. He was completely unprepared for the effect.

Pepper said absolutely nothing. She seemed transfixed, sitting as still as if an arrow were still in her and if she moved she would bleed to death.

'What?' said Steven, irritated. *'What?'*

He realised that she had whitened so much he could make out skilful make-up dusted over her perfectly bloodless cheeks. She looked sick.

There was the tiniest pause. But the silence felt as if it went on for ever. Then the host pulled himself together and moved on to the next question. Then another.

Pepper came back to life, answering her questions, even cracking a couple of jokes. But she did not meet Steven's eyes any more. And when the closing music sounded through the studio she got up and walked out without a word to anybody.

As soon as the music died Windflower came over and stood in front of him. How was it possible for a nine-year-old to have a face like a hanging judge? Steven thought, irritated.

'That lady is crying,' she announced.

Steven was harassed. 'Don't be silly,' he said. 'Grown-ups don't cry.'

Windflower gave him a look of ineffable scorn and didn't bother to reply.

He stood up and looked at the doors through which Pepper had disappeared. Was the blasted woman really *crying*? Damn! Laminated feminists weren't supposed to cry. He didn't even know what he'd done. But it was his fault; he knew that without a shadow of a doubt. If Windflower's expression hadn't told him, his own vague sense of unease would have done so.

And Martin Tammery confirmed it. The producer arrived, rubbing his hands with glee.

'Brilliant,' he said. 'Just brilliant. Couldn't be better. Come and have a drink to celebrate.'

'Celebrate?' Steven raised his brows. 'But it felt terrible.'

'Sorry about that,' said Martin, unconvincingly. He bustled him back to the subterranean hospitality room. 'Yes, Ms Calhoun turned out to be a handful, didn't she? They're all the same, these businesswomen. Trouble in pearl earrings. But on this occasion it's going to be worth it.'

Steven shook his head, bewildered.

'A spat like that is worth its weight in gold in the ratings,' Martin explained kindly. 'In fact Disgusted of Sunderland will probably have started ringing in already—' He broke off abruptly.

Pepper Calhoun had stalked into the hospitality suite with her head high and her normally soft brown eyes snapping.

Martin grabbed the programme's researcher by the elbow and hissed in her ear, 'Keep her sweet. Keep her *here*.' And ducked out of the side door before Pepper's gimlet glance could nail him to the carpet.

The researcher was a lot more nervous of Pepper than she had been before the programme. She stepped forward nervously. 'C-can I offer you something to drink, Ms Calhoun?'

If Pepper had been spiky before the recording, now she looked as if she drank hot blood. And was thirsty for a top-up *right now*.

'Water,' said Pepper grimly. 'A lot.'

Steven went over to her.

'Putting out the fire?' he drawled.

As an olive branch, it had a few design flaws. She would think he was laughing at her. He realised that the moment he said it. But it was too late to recall his words.

Pepper turned a flaming look on him.

'Anyway, it's all over,' Steven said, busily making bad worse.

'No, it's not,' said Pepper. 'It's on videotape. Highly sale-able videotape.'

Steven blinked.

'Don't worry,' said the researcher comfortingly. 'They edit a lot. They'll edit out any bad bits before they sell it on to another network.'

Pepper looked at her. 'How long have you worked here?'

'Six months,' said the researcher, flushing.

'I see,' Pepper crisply. 'Well, let me give you an insight into how the media work. When you've been here longer, you'll find out that they edit out the boring stuff. What just happened in there was not boring.'

Steven could not help himself. He laughed.

Pepper ignored him. 'In fact it's probably this crummy little outfit's passport to prime time,' she said dispassionately.

Even Steven looked disconcerted at that.

The researcher said, 'I don't understand.'

Pepper looked straight at Steven Konig. 'Bad behaviour always brings in the punters,' she said in a level voice.

The heavy eyebrows rose. 'Are you telling me off, Ms Calhoun?'

'I'm saying you could do with some lessons. In media management. In courtesy,' said Pepper, still dispassionate. And quite deadly.

His eyes flickered, as if she had struck home. But he said in a mocking voice, 'You mean you're allowed to call me a tyrant, but if I say women should take responsibility for their own wellbeing, I'm a foul oppressor?'

Her eyes flashed. But her tone stayed cool. 'I think you should have shown a little more restraint, yes.'

He snorted. 'Courtesy is supposed to go in both directions, you know.'

'I do. I was.' She took the water that the researcher poured for her and drank it down in one go. 'Unlike you.'

'How?' said Steven, exasperated. 'Why?'

'You were ungentlemanly,' she said, drawling as deliber-ately as he. 'And you know it.'

He snorted. 'If you can't stand the heat, you should have stayed out of the kitchen.'

'Oh, I can stand the heat, Professor Konig. I was brought up in the kitchen,' she said dulcetly. 'Were you?'

He looked startled. 'Is that a threat?'

Pepper permitted herself a smile. She had a wonderful smile when she wanted, and she knew it. It made her eyes dance and lit up her whole face.

'No, no,' she said, cooing like the southern belle her grandmother had always wanted her to be. 'Not a threat. A declaration of war.'

She walked out.

CHAPTER FOUR

MARTIN TAMMERY was not pleased with his assistant. 'I told you to hang on to Pepper Calhoun,' he snapped. 'How could you let her storm off like that?'

Steven's conscience stirred. No other woman was going to have grounds to call him unchivalrous today. He stepped in front of the woman.

'I'm the one you'd better yell at, Martin. We had a row, Ms Calhoun and I.'

Martin could not shout at his influential guest. 'Oh, well, I suppose it can't be helped,' he said, though not very graciously. He caught sight of Windflower, sitting watchfully in her corner, and gave a sigh of relief. 'Oh, she's left her child behind. She'll be back.'

'The child is mine,' said Steven curtly.

Martin's eyebrows flew up.

'Never mind the child. Ms Calhoun and I have unfinished business. You'd better give me her phone number.'

Martin gave a crack of laughter. 'You think she'd take a call from you? In your dreams!'

Steven was exasperated by all this emotionalism. 'Why on earth shouldn't she?'

Tammery exchanged glances with the assistant. 'Well, you did just call her a fatty on national television.'

'*What?*'

Steven's roar lifted Windflower out of her chair and brought her to his side. He put his hand on the child's shoulder absentmindedly.

'What are you talking about? I never called her anything!'

'I bet she'll blame me,' Martin pursued, not listening.

'They always do. Get themselves into a fight and, hey, presto, it's the Machiavellian producer who set it all up.'

'I'd never say a thing like that,' said Steven, really perturbed. 'Not to anyone. And, anyway, she isn't fat.'

'Well, she's a bit chubby,' said Martin fairly. 'Anyway, all women think they're fat. In fact, if it we hadn't been going out live, I bet I'd have her lawyers on the phone already.'

'Lawyers?' Steven didn't believe it. 'You're as crazy as she is.'

'Believe me, she'd have that bit edited out if she could,' Martin assured him. He looked alarmed, a sudden thought obviously striking him. 'We did get her to sign that release, didn't we?'

'What bit?' shouted Steven, stampeded into bad grammar by sheer exasperation.

The assistant did not seem to have noticed Steven's chivalrous defence. She was too agitated to pay attention to anyone but her boss.

'Yes, it's all right, Martin. We had the release last week. She sent it in with her acceptance.'

Martin gave a sigh of relief. 'Thank God for that. There will be plenty of bidders.'

Steven breathed hard. 'Now, listen to me,' he said in the voice that he had used only a couple of times in Kplant's history. Nobody who heard it ever forgot it.

It even stopped Martin Tammery for a moment. He took one look at Steven's fierce expression and decided to put an approach to the regional news programmes on hold for a while.

'Sorry,' he said. 'What is it?'

'Bidders?' said Steven in a frighteningly still voice.

'Oh, that.' Too late, Martin saw the trap in front of him. He did the best he could. 'Erm—the two of you together are really good television. Nothing like a duel for keeping the punters tuned in.'

'Punters?' echoed Steven. He looked stunned. 'That's what *she* said.'

Martin had missed Pepper's diatribe, but the assistant looked so guilty that he got the point. 'Don't get excited, Steven—'

'Oh, my God. She was right, wasn't she? You're going to splice bits together to make it look as if I did insult the woman. And then you're going to sell the damned clip to some scandal hour.'

Martin hurrumphed in deep offence. 'It's a very educational programme—'

Steven waved that aside with contempt. 'I want to see the whole recording,' he said grimly. 'From beginning to end. And I want to see it *now*.'

Martin made a valiant stand for independence. 'Not just at the moment, Steven. I've got some calls out—'

'Now,' said Steven implacably.

'I don't think you quite understand the timing constraints—'

'No. *You* don't understand, Martin. I want to see exactly what I said in there. And exactly how she reacted. Or,' Steven said quite gently, 'it won't be her lawyers you have to worry about. It will be mine.'

Martin Tammery looked at him for a long, frustrated moment. And believed him.

They watched the programme in the small viewing suite. When it finished there was total silence.

Then Steven swallowed audibly. 'Oh—my—God.'

Martin tried not to look smug. 'A duel. I told you. Great television. You are,' he added, not very tactfully but with perfect truth, 'very well matched.'

Steven ignored him. 'It wasn't my imagination,' he said almost to himself. 'She looked as if I'd hit her.'

'Very interesting bit of body language,' said Martin rising. 'I'd say she hates your guts. Now, if you'll excuse me, I've got to speak to New York.'

Steven blocked his way.

'Don't even think about it.'

'But—'

'I,' said Steven gently, 'have not signed my release form.
Sell a single centimetre of that footage and I'll sue the
Y-fronts off you.' He grasped Windflower's hand, looking
down at her remorsefully. 'I owe you an apology, too. Adults
do cry.'

She nodded, without comment.

His hold tightened. 'Come on, Windflower. You and I have
got things to put right. Lots of them.'

Pepper closed the door of the flat behind her and leaned
against it, her eyes tight shut. She was shaking. Four hours
later and still in shock, she thought dispassionately.

'Pepper?'

Her eyes flew open, startled. Normally neither of her cousins was home before seven. But Izzy was standing in the
kitchen doorway. She looked worried.

'What is it? What's happened? Has your grandmother been
making trouble again?' said Izzy in quick concern.

Pepper gave a wry smile. Izzy was a lot more right than
she could guess. Up to now it had only been Mary Ellen
Calhoun who'd sent her into this chilled, sick state.

'No,' she said dryly. 'This time it was someone else calling
me a potato. And he did it on daytime television.'

Izzy blinked. 'Potato? Television? Oh, yes, it was your
talk-show thing today, wasn't it? But I don't understand.
Why would anyone call you a potato?'

Pepper held her arms round herself protectively and
pushed her shoulders away from the door. 'That's my grandmother's word for it. It's code. Not subtle. But it sure tells
it like it is.'

Izzy frowned in concern. 'I don't understand. We call people a couch potato sometimes. It means they slob around in
front of the television and eat chips all day. No one could
say you do that.'

'What Grandmother means,' said Pepper evenly, 'is that I
need to come down three dress sizes.'

'Oh.'

'I have no idea what Lord Zog meant. Probably just trying to be nasty.' She pushed a hand through her damp hair. 'And he did it, right on the button.'

'Ouch,' said Izzy with quick sympathy. 'Who is Lord Zog? Boils on the bum to him, anyway. Come and tell all.'

Pepper allowed herself to be led into the bright, untidy kitchen. She sat at the breakfast bar and pushed the morning's mail and a bright pot plant to one side. She could not get used to her cousins' untidiness. Or the constant wicked laughter. Nobody laughed much at the Calhoun mansion. Or their easy, unspoken support for each other, though they could not have been less alike: good, lovely Jemima and wild, rule-breaking Izzy.

Now, with Izzy bustling about making her the violent orange tea that they drank all the time, quite suddenly Pepper thought, I'm one of them, too.

Her shoulders had been up round her ears. But at that thought they came down. Izzy put the mug of horrible stuff in front of her and Pepper put her hands round it. She realised that she wasn't shaking any more.

'How was the big interview?' said Izzy over her shoulder. 'Did Terry's hair artistry do the business for you? Convince them you were a babe with a heart?'

Pepper gave a sudden choke of laugher. 'Do you know? I don't know! I think it went fine.'

'Wow. Only think? I thought this was make or break time?'

'Well, I've done so many presentations to venture capitalists I know my speech backwards,' said Pepper dismissively. 'And I was so mad I forgot to be nervous.'

Izzy sat down opposite her. 'Mad because of—what did you call him? Lord Zog? Who is this man?'

'British male tyrant. Standard issue,' said Pepper grimly.

Izzy was entertained. 'So what did he do to you, exactly?'

Pepper's jaw clenched.

'He told me I was too fat. And had too much money.'

'What?'

'Right there in the studio with two cameras rolling. He said—' She broke off. 'Oh, I'm so mad I could spit.'

'I can see you are,' said Izzy, impressed. 'I hope you did.'

Pepper thought about Steven Konig's face as she left. 'I did better than that. I called him ungentlemanly,' she said with relish.

Izzy stared. 'That's telling him!' she said dryly.

Pepper came back from her pleasant memory with a jump. 'Well, he didn't like it one bit.'

'Er—Pepper, how old is this guy?'

'I don't know. Thirty-something, I guess. Why?'

'I thought he had to be seventy. Look, a today kind of guy doesn't give a hoot in hell if you call him ungentlemanly,' she explained kindly. 'That's what equality is all about. Haven't you noticed?'

Pepper thought about it. 'He cared,' she said positively.

Izzy shook her head. 'You are something else. Have you been living in a time warp or something?'

'Of course not,' said Pepper, stung. 'I just have standards.'

'You have a hole in the head,' her cousin said frankly. 'You know, Jay Jay and I were wondering why you didn't go out with any of the guys you met here. We thought maybe there was someone in New York?'

Pepper's pale skin went paler. But she didn't say anything.

Izzy sighed. 'Let me guess. He wasn't a gentleman either. Oh, Pepper, what are we going to do with you?'

Pepper swallowed. 'Give me a crash course on the dating jungle?' It was a brave attempt at humour. 'Not that potatoes have high survival expectations out there anyway.'

Izzy was shocked. 'You're not a potato,' she said vehemently. 'You're a beautiful, intelligent woman.'

'Who needs an exercise programme,' supplied Pepper broodingly.

'This guy really got to you, didn't he?'

'He had no right to say what he did. But he was not altogether wrong. I wouldn't admit that outside this room.' She looked at Izzy, half-defiant, half-sad. 'Go on. Tell me the truth. I can take it.'

Izzy moved restlessly about the kitchen, the mug of tea clasped in her hands like a protective talisman.

'I'm not the person to ask about this,' she said at last.

There was a note in her voice which startled Pepper. 'What's wrong?' she demanded.

Izzy stood at the window, looking out onto the rain-washed balcony. Pepper thought she was not going to answer.

And then she burst out, as if she could not contain it any longer, 'Haven't you noticed? Jemima never has dinner with us. Only takes coffee for breakfast.'

Pepper was taken aback. 'Well, she's a model—'

'And they have to watch their weight. I know. I know. But she hardly eats. And when she does I'm not sure how long it stays eaten,' Izzy said blackly.

Pepper was silenced, horrified.

Izzy pulled herself together with a visible effort. 'Maybe it's nothing. Over-protective older sister, probably. Forget I said anything.'

'Oh, Izzy.' Pepper was full of compassion. 'If there's anything I can do…'

Izzy gave a slightly shaky laugh. 'Just don't expect me to sympathise because some Neanderthal talks nonsense about weight, right? Even if they broadcast it worldwide it wouldn't make any difference. Every right-thinking woman will be on your side.'

Pepper smiled at her affectionately. But her smile died all too fast.

'I don't really care that much about what he said, actually. It's me. My reaction. I think I may have—not reacted well.'

Izzy was hopeful. 'You mean you kicked him where it hurts as well as saying he wasn't a gentleman?'

She laughed. But it was an effort. 'I damn near cried,' she said baldly.

Izzy knew that was no laughing matter.

'Yeah. Quite. Think about it. I go out pitching for seed

corn capital—and some clever researcher is going to say, Hey this woman is so unstable the moment she hits opposition she bursts into tears.'

Pepper lined up the pot plant dead centre of the kitchen table.

Concentrating on the task, she said, 'Would you invest in someone like that? I wouldn't.'

Izzy had never asked anyone to invest in her in her life. She tried to think of something comforting to say. It was not easy.

'Well, hey, it's only business,' she managed at last.

Pepper looked up, her brown eyes very serious.

'Not for me, it isn't, Izzy. I'm a professional or I'm *nothing*.'

Izzy was silenced.

'And damn him to hell,' said Pepper with concentrated fury, 'Lord Zog made me feel like nothing.'

Shopping for Windflower was astonishingly easy. Which was just as well, as more than half his mind was still on Pepper Calhoun.

How dared she call him ungentlemanly? Who did she think she was, with her wild hair and pugnacious chin? She had mocked him from the moment she saw him today. Calling him Lord Zog, for heaven's sake! Challenging him, too. She had no right to complain if he fought back.

But—there were still those tears. Whichever way you looked at it, they were down to him. *Hell!*

So it really was a relief that efficient Val had mapped out the shopping expedition for them precisely. Steven had no faith that he would have got through it under his own steam. Not even with a child as amazingly co-operative as Windflower.

In fact she was so co-operative Steven began to wonder if she were well. Surely children were supposed to be more— well—vocal? Friends with children spoke feelingly of sulks and squabbles. But Windflower accepted every tee shirt or pair of trousers with dumb delight.

In fact, from the moment she had discovered she could have both a pair of jeans and some shorts as well, she'd seemed to go into a trance. She did not ask for anything. She did not reject anything. She just held the clothes against her and stared in the mirror as if she were looking at Wonderland.

'You don't have to take anything you don't like, you know,' he said at last, worried by such total silence.

She was holding a blue denim waistcoat with a lone star on the pocket. At his words she looked up, her grip tightening. But she still didn't say anything.

He looked at the sub-cowboy gear doubtfully. 'Do you really like it?'

Windflower nodded vigorously, her eyes huge.

'Then—fine,' said Steven, giving up.

They bought shoes. And he was furious all over again when he found that the pair she was wearing had irreparable holes in the sole.

'Must have been like that for quite a while,' said the assistant, bringing trainers.

'Yes,' said Steven, his mouth thin. 'Throw them away.'

Afterwards he said, 'Now what? Chemist? Bookshop? Hairdresser?'

Windflower skipped a bit. 'Hairdressers are for grown-up ladies,' she said.

It sounded like a mantra she had learned a long time ago, Steven thought with sympathy.

She looked at him sideways. 'Do you like Pepper's hair?'

Steven jumped. 'What?'

'Pepper. Her hair is so cool. I wish I had hair like that. Don't you think her hair is lovely?'

He swallowed, disconcerted. Just for a few seconds his mind's eye was full of waving red curls, gleaming like fire, looking as if they would be electric to touch. He swallowed. 'I suppose so.'

'Don't you like her?'

He began to feel hounded. 'I don't know her. I like her well enough.'

Windflower did not say anything. But she had a line in silent scepticism that would do credit to a woman four times her age.

'Oh, all right, she annoyed me,' said Steven, giving in. 'Haven't you ever been annoyed with anyone?'

Windflower digested that. 'I thought she was nice.'

'Yeah. Well, maybe she is. You can't always tell with just one meeting.' He remembered his infinitely regretted shy goddess. 'Or even two.'

She walked beside him in silence for a bit.

'So—will we see her again?'

'Yes,' said Steven, with a lot more emphasis than the question demanded. 'Yes, we certainly will. And as soon as possible.'

But it was not as easy as that.

He called Indigo Television on his cellphone at once, but they were not inclined to help. Martin Tammery was still angry with him for spoiling his story and flatly refused to surrender a contact number.

'We have a duty of care to our guests,' he said pompously. 'We cannot hand out their personal details. You might be a stalker.'

Steven breathed hard. 'Martin. I have never stalked anyone in my life.'

'She still might not want to talk to you. You did,' said Martin meanly, 'call her a fat slob on air.'

Steven's control snapped. 'I did not call her a fat—' he yelled.

By this time he and Windflower were on a District Line underground train, heading towards Paddington. Their fellow passengers looked interested. Windflower drummed her heels against the seat and looked round, beaming. She seemed to enjoy the attention.

Steven moderated his voice. 'Okay. Don't give me a number. Will you just pass on a message for me?'

But Martin was unforgiving. 'I don't think that would be appropriate.'

'But she might want to talk to *me*.'

'She knows who you are. If she wants to get in touch she can call Queen Margaret's. If she doesn't, I'm not risking a mauling,' Martin said frankly. '*Goodbye*, Steven.'

So he'd have to go another way. Well, that would be okay. The woman was an entrepreneur, after all. She had to make herself available to investors. So someone would know how to contact her. How difficult could it be to track one of them down?

Over the ensuing week he found out. Very difficult indeed.

Calhoun Carter denied all knowledge of Ms Calhoun's presence in the UK. They insisted she was still in New York and recommended an e-mail to her office. The e-mail went unanswered. As did his phone calls.

So he tried the journalist who had seen her on the plane. Sandy Franks had fallen asleep at the New York conference after a particularly good lunch. His report on the afternoon session was pure fiction, primed by Steven's notes. Sandy Franks owed him.

But, even owing him, Sandy was not very helpful.

'The Tiger Cub? You're out of your depth there, old boy.'

'What do you mean?' said Steven, irritated.

'She bites,' said Sandy frankly. 'Not as lethal as her grandmother, the dreaded Mary Ellen. But coming along nicely for her age.'

'She didn't bite me.' Steven was rueful. 'Rather the reverse. I owe her an apology.'

'Then steer clear. Unless you think you can live without your liver.'

'*What?*'

'They bear grudges, the Calhouns. And they like to win. If you've beaten her at something, just thank your lucky stars and move on. Fast.'

Steven thought of the pale face, the stunned eyes. Oh, she'd thrown out a challenge afterwards, all right. Of course she had. But when he had spouted all that damned nonsense about food and excuses she had looked as if he had struck her to the heart. Not like a tiger cub who would claw his liver out. Just a wounded woman.

And he was the one who had delivered the wound. He hated that. It still brought him awake at nights. A couple of times he had heard himself shouting, *'No,'* as a dream Pepper crumbled to dust in front of his horrified eyes.

He wasn't telling anyone about that dream. Instead he said casually, 'I'd prefer to see her. Clear the air.'

'You're mad. Forget her.'

So casual didn't work. 'Sandy, this is important to me,' said Steven quietly.

The journalist sighed. 'Okay. I'll ask around. But too many people keep the Calhouns' secrets for them. If Pepper wants to maintain a low profile, I won't find her.'

And he didn't.

Steven stopped being discreet. He asked everyone he could think of if they knew Pepper Calhoun. Nobody did. Fortunately there wasn't anyone who watched daytime television either, so nobody asked why he wanted to know.

As far as he could tell, the only people who had picked up his uncharacteristic outburst were a couple of undergraduates. To his dismay, they seemed to be on his side.

'Tell it like it is,' one of them said, passing him in the chapel quad as he came back from his morning run.

'The oppressed male fights back,' said the other.

They bowed gravely and passed on.

Steven clutched his hair and pelted for his office.

'I've got a couple of young fogies thinking I'm Iron John,' he told Val, in despair.

Val had also watched the programme, out of simple loyalty. She had not said a word about it. Also out of loyalty, Steven surmised.

Now she sniffed. 'More than a couple. There's a motion

in the junior common room suggestions book to invite you and Ms Calhoun to head up the End of Term Debate.'

'Oh.' Steven thought about it. Maybe the undergraduates would have more success at tracking her down than he had. 'That sounds interesting.'

Val's face was expressionless. 'Motion: This House holds that men are always wrong.'

'*Oh,*' said Steven in quite another voice. He leaned against the corner of his desk and ran his hands through his hair distractedly. 'This is getting out of hand, isn't it?'

Valerie said carefully, 'It does seem to be preying on your mind a lot. You nearly missed three meetings yesterday. And you do know that you've got the Fund-Raising Sub-Committee in ten minutes, don't you?'

Steven was still in his running gear, with the sweat stains to prove that it was not just for show. He laughed and got to his feet.

'It's okay. I hadn't forgotten. Just cutting it a bit fine. Thank God for living above the shop.'

He ran up the spiral staircase to his private rooms, pulling his running vest off as he went. Val shook her head after him. Why did a gorgeous man like that have the worst taste in the world in women? Courtney Underwood was a disaster, but at least she was beautiful. Pepper Calhoun looked as if she would flame him if he got anywhere near her. But the man was still driving himself mad trying to find her. Crazy!

She went back to her own room, where Windflower was playing on the computer. Steven had found a school for her and the college staff were helping out as best they could.

'Finishing your homework?' asked Val, setting up for the day.

Windflower shook her head. 'Visiting my friend Pepper's website.'

'Nine-year-olds have websites now, do they?' said Val, amused. Then she did a doubletake. 'Pepper?'

She went to look. The site seemed to be telling a story of

some sort, with pictures of an old house and an orchard and a woman with wild red curls picking apples...

Steven was running lightly down the stairs, on his way to the senior common room. She put her head out of the door.

'Master, there's something here I think you should see.'

'I haven't got time—'

'I think I may have found a way of contacting Ms Calhoun.'

The Fund-Raising Sub-Committee had to wait for the Master for nearly an hour.

Out of the Attic had a great launch party. Even Pepper, who hated parties and never went to them unless she had to, agreed that it was a great party. Not a big party, but select. Everyone was there for a purpose—journalists, magazine editors, photographers. Pepper had worked hard at the guest list—and even harder at what she had to say to each one individually.

'Just my sort of party,' she told Izzy, looking round the small, full room with satisfaction.

Izzy was working full time with Pepper on *Out of the Attic* these days. She grinned. 'You mean it's all work, no play.'

Pepper was getting used to being teased. 'I mean it has focus,' she said loftily.

Jemima, adding her lustrous presence and fashion model name for free, stopped beside them for a moment.

'Everyone I've talked to is very impressed. You're going to do it, Pepper.'

Pepper nodded. 'It's looking good,' she agreed. 'Now, next I have to talk to—' She scanned the room. And stiffened abruptly. *'What is he doing here?'*

Izzy looked round, bewildered. 'Who? Where?'

'If you mean the hunk with the eyebrows,' said Jemima, 'he says you met on a plane.'

'Oh, we've met all right,' said Pepper grimly. 'Though the only thing airborne was my temper.'

The other two looked at her.

'You mean that's *him*?' Izzy was incredulous. 'How dare he show his face here?'

Jemima subjected the interloper to a dispassionate assessment. 'Looks as if he'd dare most things. You didn't say he was so sexy, Pepper.'

Her cousin's look spoke volumes. Jemima threw up her hands, laughing.

'Okay. Okay. *I* think he's sexy. You think he's a toad. What are you going to do about him?'

'Throw him out,' said Izzy with enthusiasm.

But Pepper looked at all the photographers she had invited and ground her teeth.

'We can't do that. So far no one seems to have picked up on that terrible programme. Let's keep it that way.'

'How?' asked Izzy, unversed in the codes of publicity.

Jemima, however, lived by it. 'Chat brightly. Make like he's Pepper's dearest friend. Or someone will pick up the atmosphere—and then you can say a big hello to tomorrow's headlines. Isn't that right, Pepper?'

'It's a risk,' agreed Pepper.

She narrowed her eyes. Across the room Steven Konig had accepted a glass of her champagne and was talking absorbedly to a financial columnist from one of the broadsheets. As if he felt her eyes on him, he looked up.

And raised his glass in silent toast, as if they were friends. Intimate friends. As if they were lovers.

Pepper drew a little hissing breath. Publicity or no publicity, she was going to get Steven Konig right between those devil's eyebrows. She owed it to herself and all women.

'I'll deal with this,' she said.

She walked away from her cousins without a backward look. She left them open-mouthed.

'Wow,' said Jemima. 'Fasten your seatbelts.'

Two could play at the intimacy game. Pepper went bang up to Steven Konig and gave him a warm, false smile. He looked uncertain for a moment. She was glad.

But he recovered fast. 'So you got your funding. You certainly deserve to. I looked at the website. Very intriguing. I was impressed, I admit.'

'Good,' said Pepper, keeping her bright smile in place. 'Drink to the success of *Out of the Attic* and go.'

He raised his glass to her with deep, deep mockery. 'World peace.'

Pepper's eyes glittered. She raised her glass in response. 'Boils on your bum,' she said, borrowing from Izzy, inspired. Her smile did not falter.

Steven blinked. Her smile widened to genuine delight. Across the room, the photographer aimed his camera, snapping hard. Pepper saw it. It would look as if they were flirting. Good, she thought viciously. She hoped that whoever his partner in life was, she gave him hell over it.

She leaned towards him and put a confiding hand on his arm. He had to bend his tall head to hear her.

'You bastard,' she said sweetly.

Steven's eyes gleamed. 'That's what I want to talk about.'

It was Pepper's turn to be confused. 'What?'

'Bastard I may be. Stupid I undoubtedly am. But I never meant that damned television programme to get personal.'

He looked so honest. So remorseful.

Just as well that she remembered the last man to look honest and remorseful. Ed had looked so convincing. She had thought he was a friend. And in the end he had just treated her like a commodity. She was not going to make that mistake again. Especially not with Lord Zog.

Pepper snatched her hand away from his arm. She said chattily, 'You know, men do that so well.'

He was wary. 'Do what?'

'That I'm-so-sorry-I-sold-you-down-the-river thing.'

Steven bit his lip. 'I'm sorry you think that.'

She gave a light, hard laugh. 'And then you say, everything is allowed in business.'

'No,' he said, revolted.

'And I have to learn not to be such a teen queen about it.'

Her mouth still smiled but her eyes were chips of ice. 'Am I right?'

Steven was getting his second wind. 'Of course not.'

'No?'

'No!' He was genuinely indignant. 'And what's more I think I've just been getting the speech for some other chap's prosecution.'

Pepper was taken aback.

He saw it and pressed his advantage home. 'Look, I spoke without thinking. There's some stuff going on in my private life and I—just went over the top. It was nothing to do with you, whatever it looked like.'

She sniffed. But it was difficult to stay furious in the face of such a whole-hearted climb-down.

Steven stepped closer. 'It wasn't fair. I'm really sorry.'

Pepper wavered for a moment. Maybe this was genuine. Maybe he wasn't playing some clever game with a useful commodity. Maybe—

But then he said, 'Look, have dinner with me. Let me make peace properly.'

She was tempted. She was really tempted. And in the end that was what stopped her dead in her tracks. Temptation made you vulnerable.

She thought, *Hell, it's a mercy date! He thinks I'm such a potato I'll do anything for an evening with a man.*

On pure adrenaline, she rapped out, 'No, thank you,' before she had time to think about it.

Steven was stunned. No doubt about it. His head went back as if she had hit him.

'I'm sorry?' he said blankly.

Pepper retreated, breathing hard. 'I mean no way; it's not going to happen; forget it,' she said crisply.

'But—'

'You've apologised. Thank you. Goodbye.'

His eyes narrowed in what she thought of as his Lord Zog look. 'I'm not leaving.'

Pepper narrowed her eyes right back at him. 'Oh, I think you are. This is my party, Professor Konig.'

He smiled. 'It is indeed. And stuffed to the gills with journalists. Do you really want to give them a gift like that?'

'Huh?'

Steven was amused. 'Well, put it this way. I won't go quietly.'

Their eyes locked. *Impasse.* Pepper felt her pulse beat faster... There was something about his expression... Again she had that fierce stab of memory, as if she had met him before. More, as if he were *important*.

Her face must have changed, because he closed the distance between them.

'Unless you come, too,' he said in a quick, urgent undervoice. 'In fact, why don't you do that? Come with me now. I know somewhere we can talk.'

For a moment she was tempted. For a moment she looked into his dark eyes and all she could see was Steven Konig *wanting* her. Pepper's mouth dried in a way it had not since she was a teenager.

Teenager! Teen Queen! Mercy Date!

She struggled back to the real world.

'We talked,' she said coldly. 'Not a great experience for me. I'm not standing in line to do it again.'

Even that didn't crush the man. He was as tough as an alligator—and as tricky.

'You're missing a good thing.' And he was *smiling*. As if she were a child having a tantrum—and would know better in a while!

A red mist came up before Pepper's eyes. She heard herself say, 'Okay, if that's what you want. Stick around. Get loaded on my champagne. Enjoy yourself.'

'Thank you. I will. I am.' Laughter bubbled in his voice.

She ignored that. 'Just keep away from me. Come near me again and I'll throw something. Journalists, cameras—they can go jump! I'm warning you.'

'Thank you,' said Steven gravely. But his eyes danced.

Pepper nearly emptied her glass over his head there and then. Only the thought that he would probably find that funny too stopped her.

She made a noise like an infuriated wasp and turned on her heel.

She was shaken. She had never lost her cool like that before. She was Penelope Anne Calhoun, the coolest head on campus, the girl who had gone to business receptions before she was out of hair ribbons. Yet she had forgotten her upbringing. Even forgotten what was at stake at this party. Just for a moment, all she had wanted to do was upend her glass of champagne over Steven Konig's laughing face and dance with rage.

She was disgusted with herself. She was behaving like some society beauty having a spat with a regency rake, instead of a responsible twenty-first-century businesswoman.

Izzy came over, concerned. 'What is it?'

'This crazy country. It's getting to me,' Pepper muttered.

Izzy looked past her shoulder. 'Ah,' she said. 'Just the country? That's a man on the prowl, if ever I saw one.'

Pepper refused to look. 'You're joking.'

Izzy pursed her lips. 'Sexy, too. Maybe it's time to play again? Just a little? I mean now that you know where you're going, with *Out of the Attic* up and running, you'd have a bit more time.'

Pepper was outraged. 'Don't even go there. That is *so* not going to happen.'

Izzy was alarmed. After all, she worked for Pepper now. She had been looking forward to a summer that was more relaxed than the last hectic weeks.

She said reproachfully, 'You said once we'd got the first phase funding…'

Pepper waved it aside. 'That's just the start. I told you. I'm a woman on a mission. *No one* is going to get in my way. Especially not Lord Zog.'

And she stamped off to do some serious sucking up to one of her targeted editors.

She had been working the room hard for more than an hour by the time Martin Tammery arrived. She was talking to Sandy Franks, one of the best-connected financial stringers in London. They both looked up as Martin waved ostentatiously.

'Pepper!' he called, heading towards them.

Sandy Franks raised his eyebrows. 'You're on first-name terms?'

'I went on his programme. I guess any guest who doesn't end up suing him becomes a long-term buddy,' said Pepper dryly.

'Oh, this new thing of his. *In My Experience*. I heard about that.' He looked at her shrewdly. 'Got yourself in a bit of a pickle, I'm told.'

She stiffened. 'Oh?'

'They say you went head to head with Steven Konig over a woman's right to neurosis,' said Sandy Franks, unperturbed.

Pepper's polite smile was rigid. 'That's one way of putting it.'

He stopped teasing and grinned. 'No need to look like that. People were bound to tell me. I'm too well connected. I doubt if anyone else in this room has heard a whisper. They don't watch daytime television. And Indigo won't run it again. Or sell on clips, either, from what I've heard.'

She was still as tense as a steel hauser, but she frowned, momentarily distracted. 'What makes you think that?'

'Steven Konig put the fear of God into Tammery. And the board of Indigo, too, I hear.'

'*What?*' Pepper stared. '*Steven Konig* stopped them passing it round? I don't believe you! I haven't heard anything about it.'

Franks' grin widened. 'I told you. I'm very well connected. I hear everything.'

She shook her head slowly. 'But why would he bother? He wasn't the one who looked like a total loser.'

'Who knows? Maybe he has a conscience,' said Franks

airily. Steven had tracked him down only ten minutes ago and primed him comprehensively. 'Better take it up with him yourself.'

Pepper's expression answered for her.

Poor old Steven, thought Sandy Franks. The Tiger Cub was going to see the colour of his liver before she went to the funfair with him. But Steven was a mate. He would do his best for him.

'He's a good guy, you know. Principled. Could be a multimillionaire but he isn't. His share of the profits of Kplant go into a trust fund to educate third-world farmers.'

She showed no sign of being impressed. Sandy Franks sighed. Well, she wouldn't be, would she? She was a profit-orientated capitalist down to her gleaming fingernails.

He said, 'Give the guy a break, Pepper.'

Then Martin Tammery was upon them. Franks gave up. He stayed just long enough for a polite few words with him and moved on. He headed for the door and the next party on his evening engagement list.

'Forget it, old chum,' he said in Steven's ear as he passed. 'It's hopeless. Women just don't listen.'

Steven looked across the room at Pepper. She was laughing at something that someone had said to her, and just for a moment she looked like his golden goddess again.

'I don't believe that,' he said. 'I won't believe that. I'll get through to her somehow.'

Franks pulled a face. 'Rather you than me. You'll never get that one to climb down. Take it from a veteran dater of professional women.'

But he was wrong.

When the party was down to friends and family and the most determined party animals, Pepper made an unexpected move. Watching her, as he had watched all evening, Steven saw her put down her glass, brace herself, and turn resolutely. She marched across the floor as if she were going to face a firing squad. And she was coming to him.

Steven went towards her. They met in the middle of the

room. There was no one near. They might just as well have been on their own.

Pepper's chin was at a dangerous angle.

'They tell me you stopped the broadcast.' She shot it out at him like a duellist's challenge.

He said gently, 'I stopped secondary sales, yes.'

He thought she would ask how. Entrepreneurs were always interested in how you made the media do things.

She didn't. She said fiercely, *'Why?'*

He didn't answer for a moment. Her eyes were huge—brown and bewildered and determined, not to be sold a line. Steven wanted to kiss her.

'Because of me?' she said furiously. 'There was no need.'

He spread his hands.

'I didn't cry, you know. I don't care what people think they saw. *I did not cry!'*

'Of course not.'

The soothing tone was a mistake. She glared at him.

'I don't need special handling. I can take care of myself.'

Her eyes snapped. He wanted to take her in his arms and kiss her until her eyes closed and she melted against him...

He swallowed. 'I know you don't.'

'So why interfere?'

Steven said carefully, 'I was unchivalrous. You weren't expecting an attack. Result—both of us looked—' he considered and discarded all the words she would resent '—unimpressive,' he concluded.

Pepper stared.

Not very encouraging, Steven thought. He tried a winning smile. 'Neither you nor I needed that. All I've done is to make sure that revealing clips don't haunt us in the future as we go onward and upward.'

The wide brown eyes were unwinking. He could not tell what she was thinking. Oh, hell, he hadn't sounded as if he were patronising her, had he?

She put her head on one side. 'So you're saving your own face as much as mine?' she asked in a neutral voice.

'Yes,' he said fervently.

A huge smile broke through. And that divine shyness that he remembered. She was slightly pink about the cheekbones and her voice was gruff.

'Liar. But thank you.' She thrust out her hand. 'My turn to apologise, I think.'

So she wouldn't climb down, huh? Sandy Franks, you're an idiot. This is a woman who wants her men to be gentlemanly. This is a woman of principle.

He felt as if a dark prison had suddenly collapsed like a house of cards, without him having to do a thing about it.

He took her hand and held on to it. 'Then do it properly. Have dinner with me.'

Her fingers twitched in his hold. 'I—'

'Go on. What have you got to lose?' He laughed down into her. 'Let's share the heat of the kitchen and see where it gets us.'

CHAPTER FIVE

STUPID, stupid, *stupid.* Steven cursed himself all the way back on the train to Oxford.

Of course she wouldn't come out to dinner with him. It must have sounded as if he was barely going to let the Lobster Thermidor touch her lips before he jumped on her. No woman in her right mind went to dinner with an incipient sex maniac. And Pepper Calhoun was certainly in her right mind.

The trouble was, when she got that faint flush along her cheekbones—and those glorious lashes trembled—and her voice went as gruff as a guilty schoolboy's...

Remembering was too much for his self-command. Steven gritted his teeth and concentrated hard on the shadowed landscape beyond the window until he was in control again.

Heaven help him, when Pepper Calhoun was agitated every little thing she did had the unfortunate effect of bringing his animal self banging out of the basement roaring. And Steven had thought his animal self was well and truly dead and buried, along with acne and examinations.

What on earth had he been thinking of? He had never behaved like that before. Even when he was head over heels in love with Courtney he had never invited her to dinner in a voice that was more than half a threat.

'Captain Blood strikes again,' he said aloud.

Fortunately the carriage was empty. But the sound of his own voice startled him enough to bring him to his feet. He prowled restlessly along the aisle, backwards and forwards, backwards and forwards, his mind racing.

What had the woman *done* to him?

And what in the world was he going to do about it?

*   *   *

Stupid, stupid, *stupid*. Pepper could not keep her mind on the cheerful conversation.

Jemima had booked a table at a fashionable Italian bistro for dinner after the reception. 'There are always stragglers,' she had said wisely.

She was right. The rump of the party was not going to be moved without offer of some serious protein. They were full of champagne and goodwill. *Out of the Attic* ought to get a terrific press out of it.

But Pepper could have screamed with frustration. All through the endless meal she kept thinking, What am I doing here? I could be with him.

It would have been so easy to have dinner with him. After all that champagne she needed to eat. Why not with Steven Konig? The cousins could have fielded the stragglers easily.

It would have been the ideal opportunity for Pepper to make her point—and then a graceful apology on both sides, followed by a firm farewell. Closure—that was what it would have given her. And, boy, did she need closure with Steven Konig. At least she did if she were to stop thinking about him like this, all the time.

So what on earth had made her go into full retreat, like a high school girl asked on her first date? He must have thought she was a complete idiot.

Rightly, Pepper told herself grimly. She *was* a complete idiot.

Her spaghetti carbonara lost its appeal. She pushed it away.

'You and Jemima are going to break the chef's heart between you,' said Izzy dryly.

Jemima had stirred her salade niçoise around her plate, but the pile of salad leaves had not diminished much. Pepper guessed that she had eaten a mouthful of tuna and a couple of olives. No wonder Izzy was worried, she thought, startled.

But Jemima was not interested in discussing food.

'I thought your Lord Zog was great, Pepper. One for the list.'

The sisters claimed to maintain a list of eligible men. They called it the Endangered Species list.

Pepper frowned. She did not like Steven Konig. He made her feel out of control and defensive. But she did not want her glamorous cousins to hurt him.

'Leave him alone, Jay Jay.'

Her cousin looked hurt. 'I don't poach.'

'It's not a question of poaching,' said Pepper furiously. 'I just don't want to be the one to put him in the target zone.'

Izzy and Jemima looked at each other. 'What are you talking about?'

'Target zone?'

'Your seek and seduce mission,' said Pepper with feeling. 'You're lethal, both of you.'

They weren't hurt. They weren't shocked. They laughed and called her a scaredy cat.

'That's what all women do,' Jemima pointed out. 'Why should Steven Konig get special treatment?'

'Sweet. She wants to protect him,' said Izzy kindly. She shook her head. 'When will you learn, Pepper? Men don't want to be protected.'

Pepper stared.

Izzy took on her tutorial voice. 'Men think they're lords of the universe. Let a guy think you want to stop him being hurt, and he'll find it the biggest turn-off in the world.'

'Like I care,' flashed Pepper. 'I never wanted to turn Lord Zog on, if you remember.'

They both hooted. And then the subject of Steven Konig was overtaken by more important stuff, like how many people it took to order a zabaglione.

But when they got back to the apartment Pepper said quietly, 'I'm serious, guys. Leave the man alone. He's not your style.'

Jemima kicked off her five-inch heels and flung herself on the sofa. 'But he's yours.'

'No!' said Pepper recoiling.

Izzy was peeling off everything, down to her lime-green

underwear. It was a hot night. She was quite unselfconscious. More, she looked as if she was enjoying herself, dancing around bare-legged and gorgeous in her uplift bra and matching tanga.

Pepper thought, Would my self-confidence get a boost from psychedelic underwear? She thought of her abundant flesh and flinched.

Izzy rolled her party gear into a bundle, as if she were going off to swim, and lobbed it into the corner.

'Course he is. Just as well,' she added irrepressibly. 'You haven't taken to any of the men that we've trotted past you.'

'You've what?'

The sisters looked at each other and laughed. 'She didn't even notice,' sighed Jemima.

'Told you,' agreed Izzy.

Pepper was horrified. 'You've been trying to set me up with dates?'

'Sure,' said Izzy.

Pepper began to walk up and down agitatedly. 'I thought I'd got away from all that. How could you?'

The others looked at each other, bewildered.

'We do it all the time,' said Jemima eventually. 'Girls do.'

'Not this girl.' Pepper was very angry. But she could see they did not understand. She took a deep breath. 'Look, I appreciate the thought. But you two are different from me,' she said with care. 'I've dated in the past but—well, it was all very low-key. Do you know what I mean?'

They both frowned. Jemima looked embarrassed. Izzy, true to form, was more blunt. 'Do you mean you're a virgin?'

Pepper flushed. When would she get used to the frankness with which these two discussed their private lives? 'That's not quite what I meant,' she said with dignity.

'Okay. Explain, then.'

Pepper marshalled her thoughts. 'Look, there are two ways to find a boyfriend, right? Either you're both in the same group or the girl is such a spectacular dish that the tomcats just gather.'

Izzy gave a choke of laughter. 'That's one way of putting it.'

'Well, I wasn't either of those things. I've never been beautiful. And I sometimes thought I went to a different school every year. Summer camp, too. Even when I went to the local high school eventually I had a social life but— Well, let's just say I was not the cheerleader type.'

'You were a swot,' Izzy interpreted comfortingly. 'So was Jay Jay. People grow out of it.'

Pepper was surprised into laughing in spite of herself. 'I guess they do, at that.'

Izzy's comforting tone became edged with impatience. 'So, when you were sixteen you were a swot, not a swinger. What has that got to do with the price of fish?'

This was so much more difficult than she could have imagined. She could not bring herself to share her cousins' frankness. She imagined herself saying, I got dates because the boys in high school were all the sons of people who owed my grandmother, and she came out in a cold sweat. Was she ever going to get over the effect Mary Ellen had had on her life? *You have no idea what it cost me to get you a social life.*

She said, 'I did get dates. I went to parties and picnics. But—take the high school prom. There was always a guy to escort me. But at the end of the evening people stop clowning around. That's when it gets up close and personal, you know?'

They were both staring at her as if they had been stuffed.

'The slow dance moment?' said Pepper desperately.

'You mean when someone turns the lights out and everybody goes into a clinch?' said Izzy gropingly.

'Not at any school I ever attended,' said Pepper, shocked into laughter for the second time. 'But in principle, yeah, you've got it.'

Both cousins still looked blank.

'And?' prompted Izzy.

'I pretended I was enjoying myself,' said Pepper baldly.

There was a pause. The cousins looked at each other.

Then Izzy patted her hand. 'Yup. Women do that. It's only adolescent males who think sex is a group sport.'

'But that's just the point,' said Pepper sorrowfully. 'The guy was pretending, too. In fact—'

In fact he probably had a contract with my grandmother in his pocket. No, she was not going to say that. Not even to these unshockable cousins. She needed to hang on to some self-respect, after all.

'Look, guys, I really appreciate what you're trying to do. But just leave it, okay? I've had steady dates in the past and I know I'm better off without them. Believe me.'

She tried to sleep but it was fitful. In the end she gave up and padded out into the kitchen. She even made herself some of their disgusting orange tea, though she could not bring herself to put milk in it.

Oh, it was not *fair*. She should be on top of the world. She had her start-up funding. Now she could rent the Victorian shop she had found; confirm her orders with the suppliers; start to plan the opening. She was on her way at last, doing what she did best.

And all she could do was sit here in the dark thinking about a man she had met twice in her life.

This is no time to turn into a kid with a crush, she scolded herself. Grow up. You're responsible for other people's money here.

Yes, that was better. When self-contempt did not work, guilt was always a great spur, she thought, mocking herself. She began to flick through the second stage of her business plan in a desultory way.

Yes, it stood up really well. Pepper was pleased. She was particularly proud of her analysis of the best locations for branches of *Out of the Attic*. It was all in there: demographics, local facilities, ambience, transport. Even the way the pattern of visitors to the area varied over the course of the day.

'The second store is even more important than the first in many ways. To minimise the impact on management it should be sited no more than two hours' journey from the first,' she had written. So what was she going to do about it?

She reviewed her list of possibles; so far she had worked on statistical information alone. Now she had better start looking at them in earnest. Where to start? St Albans? Esher? Oxford...

Oxford. It set off a warning bell in her head. Rapidly followed by an earthquake.

She remembered the nearly bearded pirate on the plane laughing down at her. His eyes. His hands. That long moment when she had thought he could hear her thoughts.

She heard herself saying, 'That's a great marketing job you're doing. Has the town got you on a retainer?'

The pirate had offered her the full Oxford tour, hadn't he? *And he was Steven Konig.*

The report fell to the floor as Pepper jumped up, hands to her cheeks. Horrified. Ashamed. *Mad.*

Oh, God, she was more than stupid. How on earth had she missed that before?

The kitchen door opened and Izzy trailed in, yawning.

'Hi,' she said. 'You all right?'

Pepper did not respond. Steven Konig was the pirate who had said 'I bet you could do just about anything you set your mind to.' The first time she'd met him she had felt as if they were two ends of an electric arc. She had wanted him to ask her name so badly. Only he hadn't. And now...

Her whirling thoughts skidded to a sickening halt. *Did he know?*

He had to know. He had turned into someone else when they met at Indigo. Pepper had not expected to see the pirate, so of course she had not recognised him. She had been deceived by the lack of beard and the casual clothes. Steven Konig in a suit was an entirely different class of renegade.

But Pepper had been just the same. Heck, she only had one wardrobe. She didn't change like a chameleon. He must have recognised her the moment he saw her. Of course he knew.

So why…?

'You don't look all right.' Izzy slumped into the kitchen chair opposite her. 'What got you out of bed at five in the morning? Hangover? Or cold feet about what you've taken on?'

Pepper's lips felt numb. 'I know who Steven Konig is.'

Izzy raised her eyes to the ceiling. 'Memory loss, too, huh? That sounds like hangover double plus. Yes, duckie, we all know who Steven Konig is. Sexy article who gave you a bad time on network television.'

'No. Well, yes, but that's not all.' Pepper raised shocked eyes. 'I met him before, Izzy. How could I have forgotten?'

Izzy blinked. 'What?'

Pepper explained. 'The guy looked like he was a member of a heavy metal band,' she finished.

She thought about his three days' growth of beard and that devil-may-care swagger. If Izzy thought he was sexy in suit, what would she have made of that? Just the thought of it made Pepper uncomfortably hot.

'I mean, not at all the sort of man who attracts me normally.'

'And that would be…?' said Izzy politely.

Pepper ignored that. 'But the plane banked and I fell. He sort of caught me, you know? And I just felt—'

'Whoosh!' supplied Izzy, whizzing her hands up like an exploding rocket.

Pepper was disturbed. 'I suppose so.' A muscle worked in her cheek. She felt irritated with herself. 'It's so not me. So—adolescent.'

'Lucky you,' said Izzy, unimpressed. 'Especially as the world clearly went whoosh for him, too.'

Pepper was torn between hope and a curious reluctance. 'You don't mean that,' she said hopefully.

'Listen, I've been watching men pant after Jemima since she was twelve. Trust the Izzy eye. That was a man on a major frustration trip last night.' Izzy beamed. 'And gorgeous with it. Great. Go for it.'

'But I don't know *how*,' Pepper wailed, shocked into simple truth.

Izzy stayed calm. 'You're quite sure you're not a virgin?'

'Absolutely. I was large. I was homely. I was a swot with a protective grandmother and a homework habit,' said Pepper coldly. 'I was not a prisoner. I'm not a virgin.'

Although the way she felt now she might just as well be. And her sexual experience was very limited in comparison with most of her generation. With her cousins', for example. She nearly admitted it. But what would be the point?

Izzy shrugged.

Pepper pounded her fists on the wall. 'Oh, why is this happening now? I haven't got time for all this. I've got a business to set up.'

'The timing is always wrong,' Izzy said tolerantly.

Pepper stiffened. 'Timing of what?'

Her cousin gave her a wide, understanding smile. 'The extremity of lust,' she said cheerfully.

Pepper flinched.

Izzy got up. 'It won't go away, you know. Better get it sorted once and for all. Before it takes over your life.'

Steven was having a difficult morning. He'd overslept, which meant that he'd had to curtail his morning run. He hadn't even had time to change out of his running gear before he got Windflower's breakfast.

She sat at the breakfast bar, swinging her legs. In her school uniform checked dress she looked the picture of wholesome innocence. Steven had learned to distrust that look.

'What is it?' he said suspiciously.

'Nothing.' She attacked her cornflakes. 'Have you done my name badge for sports day?'

'What?' Steven poured coffee, distracted.

'I *told* you. I've got to have a name badge. With my name

on it. My full name.' In case he hadn't understood, she spelled it out. 'Both bits. You said you'd do it on the computer.'

'Oh, that.' He pushed his hand through his hair. 'We'll ask Val.'

Windflower rocked complacently. 'Val can't do it.'

'She can if I ask her,' Steven said carelessly. He leaned against the counter, inhaling coffee. Pure caffeine rush. By golly, he needed it. How on earth was he going to get Pepper Calhoun to give him another chance?

'No, she can't. She tried.' Windflower's voice rose to a classic wail. 'I've got to have a badge. I've got to. *I've got to.*'

Steven looked up sharply. This was out of character. 'Calm down. Of course you'll have a badge if you need one. Why couldn't Val do it?'

Windflower's wails stopped with suspicious promptness. 'My name is too long,' she announced.

Steven saw that she was dry-eyed. He began to see where this was going.

'I see. And have you got a solution?'

Windflower pursed her lips. 'I think,' she said judicially, 'that I prob'ly ought to have a special name for school. I think that would be best.'

'Ah.'

'A short name.'

He nodded, keeping his mouth serious. 'So it would fit onto the badge. Good thinking. Any suggestions?'

Windflower shook her head, all silent virtue.

Their eyes met. Each of them was perfectly well aware of what the other was doing. And wasn't going to give an inch.

Steven was the first to break. He burst out laughing. 'All right. I'll think about it, you baggage.'

She grinned engagingly as she got off the stool. 'Thank you.'

One of the mothers gave Windflower a lift into school. Steven always walked her to the porter's lodge and handed her over. Of course normally he was not wearing running shorts and a sweat-stained tee shirt, but that couldn't be helped.

'What are you doing today?'

'French and dancing,' said Windflower, concentrating on the stuff she liked. 'And I'm sleeping over with Sarah.'

Steven was touched. It was quite clear that until she arrived in Oxford Windflower had never had a friend her own age. She had taken to pre-teen sleepovers like a man with a hangover to coffee. Worried about the impact on her friends' parents, Steven had rationed her to one a week. As a result she had a diary full of engagements stretching through to the autumn.

'Have a good time.'

'Uncle Steven…?'

'Yes?'

'Could my friends sleep over one weekend?'

His heart sank. It was only fair; he could see that. But the thought of organising nine-year-olds in the rickety Master's Lodging filled him with dread. I need a co-parent, he thought. And instantly wondered how Pepper Calhoun would handle a contained nine-year-old.

Forget it, he told himself. That's pure fantasy.

Aloud he said, 'We'll see.'

It was a glorious summer morning. The lawns glowed. The college basked. Sunshine struck gold and honey from stone buttresses on the medieval chapel. Even the gargoyles looked as if they were about break into a dance.

Steven thought of all the repairs that the building needed and his heart sank. But this was too good a morning to be in despair. On a morning like this he could even believe he would find a way through to Pepper Calhoun's guarded heart.

Beside him, Windflower said in a pleased voice, 'There's Pepper. Hello, Pepper.' She let go his hand and broke into a run.

Steven, by contrast, stopped dead. It wasn't. It couldn't be. It was.

Coming out of the porter's lodge, with her glorious hair flipping around her in the morning breeze, was his shy goddess. Not that she looked shy at the moment. Uncomfortable, wary and tough, yes. Shy, no.

And distinctly winded as the child launched herself into her.

'Hello.' She touched the child's hair awkwardly, as if she was not quite sure of the form but was secretly rather pleased. 'How are you?' It was aimed at both of them.

Steven felt a smile break out from his feet upwards. It felt as if his whole body was grinning like an idiot. For two pins he would have joined the gargoyles on the chapel and jigged round the tower.

Careful, he told himself. Careful. One wrong move and she'll take off again.

Curbing every instinct he had, he strolled over.

'I'm great,' he said. 'Windflower's on her way to school, but apart from that she's great, too. You?'

'I'm good.'

She fell silent, looking about her. Looking everywhere but at him, in fact. Oh, yes, she was definitely uncomfortable.

Oh, heavens, when she looked like that...

Steven wanted to reassure her so badly it was like a burn. But how do you reassure a prickly woman on the look-out for insults? Who challenges you as soon as look at you?

Keep those instincts under control, Konig!

He said carefully, 'This is a nice surprise.' In spite of himself, his tone was tender. 'What brings you to Oxford?'

She risked a quick glance at him then, but looked away at once before his eyes could snare hers. Was it his imagination or did a faint colour touch her pale cheekbones?

The porter came to the door of the lodge. 'Mrs Lang is here for the little girl, Master.'

He brought his mind back to practicalities. 'Thank you, Mr Jackson. Windflower, time to go.'

She let go reluctantly. 'Will you come to sports day, Pepper?'

Pepper was clearly at a loss. Steven rescued her.

He said firmly, 'We'll talk about it. Don't keep Mrs Lang waiting.'

Windflower nodded. 'I'm on the high jump team,' she said enticingly.

She held up her face to her visitor and, when Pepper seemed not to know how to respond, hauled her face down for a brisk kiss before going back to Steven for her farewell hug.

'Goodbye, baggage,' he said. 'Have a good sleepover. See you tomorrow.'

She went.

Pepper was looking stunned. 'High jump?' she echoed faintly.

Steven smiled. 'Until a couple of weeks ago Windflower lived a footloose life. No settled school. No family. She feels she's got a lot to catch up on. So she's drumming up a club to go and cheer any time she does anything. Don't let her get to you.'

'I can relate to that. But she sounds more constructive than I was.'

Steven was rueful. 'She's constructive all right. Currently she's negotiating for a name-change.'

Pepper smiled suddenly, that wonderful smile he had dreamed of. Full of warmth, just as he remembered. Full of fugitive fun, too, as if she were surprised at herself.

'Are we talking blackmail, by any chance?'

'Well, high-pressure salesmanship, certainly,' said Steven, delighting in her. 'So—what *are* you doing in Oxford? I don't flatter myself that you've come just to see me.'

Incomprehensibly, that seemed to upset her. She swallowed audibly.

'Um—'

When she swallowed Pepper's throat moved convulsively. It fascinated him. He wanted to tip her head back, so that amazing hair flowed over his pillow, red as the dawn. He wanted to kiss the length of that long ivory throat and...

Whoa, there Captain Blood! Don't forget the time and place! You can't carry her off under the nose of a nine-year-old, four students and the college porter. However much you want to!

To take his mind off his fantasies, Steven did an energetic jog on the spot. He must look an idiot, but it was better than going into the full sex maniac routine, he thought wryly.

'Can it be that you've changed your mind?'

She tensed. 'What?'

'Want to talk to me after all?' he asked gently.

She moistened her lips. Steven's temperature went up a couple of degrees. This was becoming unmanageable.

'Let's go inside and discuss it,' he said hastily. 'Have you had breakfast?'

'No. I—'

'Then let's go.'

'No, really. I don't need anything.'

He did not risk touching her. But he swept his arm round the curve of her back, as if he was pressing the air behind her to urge her forward. Pepper gave a voluptuous shiver, as if he had touched her exactly as his fantasies suggested.

Steven gave a laugh that was half a groan. 'Coffee, then,' he said. 'If you don't need it, I do.'

Pepper was finding this more difficult than she would have believed possible. She did not know what she had thought she would say to him. But nothing was as she expected.

The child was a shock. The way he looked even more so.

The child clearly lived with him. He treated her with the easy authority of a father. So was 'Uncle Steven' just a polite story?

And as for the way he looked! Pepper felt every hair on her body stand up and surrender. In a sweat-stained tee shirt and shorts, all bare tanned legs and wind-ruffled hair, he exuded sheer animal energy. And she wanted him.

It made it difficult to concentrate. It also made it all the more unbelievable that she hadn't recognised him before. The pirate was unmistakable.

He took her under a low stone arch, through a narrow alley between two stone buildings, into a quadrangle and out under a grander arch to—well, a fairy story.

'That's Rapunzel's turret!' exclaimed Pepper, stopping dead.

'Master's Lodging,' said Steven with inexplicable indifference. 'Actually, it's my office as well. Pressure on accommodation.' He held the weathered oak door open to allow her to pass through. 'Works quite well, but my secretary sees more of my private life than she wants.'

As if to illustrate that, a pleasant-faced woman came out onto the staircase.

'Good morning, Master. The Dean has rung asking for a word before the Fund-Raising Committee.'

'That man needs to get a life,' muttered Steven. 'Better fit him in, though. Anything else, Val?'

The secretary looked pointedly at his running gear. 'Nothing that can't wait until you're dressed.'

Steven laughed. 'Point taken. I'll just give my guest a coffee.'

He introduced them. The secretary acknowledged it. She looked wooden.

'Give me half an hour,' he said, leading the way to the stairs.

'Certainly, Master.' She went back into her room and closed the door on them with point.

Pepper refused to be intimidated. 'They call you Master?' She didn't believe it.

His eyes danced. 'Goes with the job. Come on.' He ran lightly up the ancient staircase.

Pepper followed more sedately. 'But *Master*!' She shook her head. 'It's feudal.'

'Oxford is good at names. The students call me King Kong,' Steven said ruefully. 'They say it's because of my eyebrows. But I'm not convinced.'

Neither was Pepper, looking at the bunching of powerful muscles under thin cotton as he led her through the door into his private rooms. She tried hard not to think about it.

'Kitchen,' said Steven, waving a hand at a bright room with an elderly wooden table and appliances that looked nearly as antique as the staircase. 'Help yourself to coffee. I'll be back.'

He went, pulling the stained tee shirt over his head. Pepper averted her eyes. But not before she had seen a hair-roughened chest and a stunningly solid pair of shoulders. The man had to work out. Was he vain? Somehow she didn't think so. It would have been easier to deal with him if she did, she thought, irritated. But at the moment he just looked too damn close to perfection: gorgeous, intelligent, successful and good with children.

Out of my league, even if I had a league, she told herself. She had never been attracted to muscle-bound men. The captain of the football team had left her cold. Monstrous biceps and sculpted abs made her feel slightly ill. But Steven's bas relief musculature made a vein throb in her temple and her arms reach on auto pilot.

She put her hands behind her like a schoolgirl.

Oh, Lord, she thought. This is what Izzy calls the extremity of lust. Gulp!

She kept her hands behind her until he had clattered up the next flight of stairs and she heard the door shut behind him.

The coffee maker was more than half full. She poured a mug and tossed it down like medicine. Coming here was a mistake. But now she had done it she had to see it through.

She could do it. Of course she could. She had confronted Ed Ivanov with his mercy dates, hadn't she? If she could do that she could face anything, no matter how unflattering.

So when Steven came back she burst into rapid speech. She spoke uninterrupted for ten minutes, her words tumbling over themselves in agitation. When she had finished he looked at her incredulously.

'You have only just remembered me from the plane, fair enough. But you want *me* to apologise to *you* because you didn't recognise me? How do you work that out?'

Pepper had not come here intending to demand an apology. But in the heat of the moment that was how it had come out, and she wasn't backing down. She said hotly, 'Because you didn't tell me you were the guy from the plane. You knew the moment we met at Indigo Television. Didn't you?'

'Not the *moment*,' he demurred. 'You were wrapped up like Nanook of the North, if you remember.'

Pepper refused to be sidetracked. 'Tell the truth.'

He pulled a wry face. 'Okay. I knew.'

'So why didn't you tell me?'

He helped himself to coffee, shrugging. 'Obviously I'd made less of an impression on you than you had on me. It happens.'

Pepper narrowed her eyes at him. 'Liar.'

He laughed. 'Well, it wasn't much of a first meeting, after all.'

Wasn't it? Pepper flinched inwardly. So the magnetic attraction had been one-sided after all! She had got it wrong again.

Well, what else could she expect? She was the woman who had thought Ed Ivanov dated her because he liked her!

What is wrong with me? she thought. She was supposed to be so intelligent! She could add up forward projections for her business plan until they were coming out of her ears. But ask her to add one man and one woman and she could not get the answer right. She could speak French and Spanish, but when it came to the language between men and women she didn't know what the words meant.

Izzy and Jemima did it on pure instinct. So did every other woman she knew. Mary Ellen had to be right. She was a freak!

She looked round for her bag. 'I must be going,' she said in a suffocated voice. 'I've got some business premises to look at.'

Steven found her bag. But he did not give it to her. Instead, he held on to it and said easily, 'If you're going to be around Oxford anyway, why don't we get together later?'

In spite of herself, a quick laugh lit Pepper's eyes. 'Sports day?'

He smiled back. It was a heady feeling.

'That's an idea. But not until the end of the month. I was thinking more of a spot of tourism. That's how I lured you down here after all.'

Pepper jumped. 'You didn't lure me down here,' she said loudly. Too loudly.

The smile in his eyes deepened. 'I tried. If you remember the plane, you must remember that. So, what about if I take you round a couple of colleges? We could go up St Mary's for the panorama. Or the river.'

'That's very kind of you but—' She was arrested. 'The river? You mean like *The Wind in the Willows*? Oh, how I loved that book. My parents used to read it to me together. It's about the only thing I can remember of them. They were supposed to be reading to me but I think actually they were reading it to each other.'

She smiled reminiscently. It was an old picture, the three of them on a beach somewhere—Brazil? The Caribbean?—with her sitting between them and her father and mother passing the book between them, stopping only to tickle her or bury her legs in the sand.

Her eyes softened. 'It was always a perfect day.'

Steven looked at her curiously. But his voice was deeply amused when he said, 'I wasn't exactly thinking of Ratty and friends. In Oxford the male student does his courting on the river.'

Courting? Pepper's spine stiffened as if someone had pulled a lever suddenly.

Steven did not appear to notice. He was saying reflectively, 'Umm, long tradition. If you're serious about a girl, you take her out in a punt, moor under a willow and read her something libidinous.'

'O-oh?' Pepper wondered if she were blushing and decided not to think about it too closely. 'Does it work?'

His grin widened. 'You can't expect me to tell you that.'

Oh, Lord, here was more of that secret language she didn't understand! She said with constraint, 'What do you mean?'

His eyes danced. 'In the battle of the sexes you're on the other side.'

She moistened her lips. He watched as if he were fascinated. Pepper didn't care if she was blushing. Inwardly she was melting. How did the man *do* that?

So, okay, she didn't speak the language. Okay, she had never done any of this sexy, teasing flirtation in her life. But she had her pride. If other women could do it, so could she. Steven Konig was not going to tie her up in knots without her at least trying to fight back.

She gave him what she hoped was a smouldering look. 'You mean I have to do my own reconnaissance?'

'I look forward to it.'

Pepper choked.

He gave her a wide, innocent look. But she was sure that he knew the effect he had on her. Steven Konig *did* speak the language. No doubt about that.

'Come on,' he said. 'Let's go and check the diary. We'll fix a time and I'll come and find you, if you give me the address. It's just the day for the river.'

He didn't say it was just the day for seduction, and she had no idea whether it was part of the package. As she followed him back downstairs Pepper made a discovery. She didn't care. She would go out with Steven Konig and she would take her chances!

His office was a strange mixture of high tech—computers and scanners abounded—and Jane Austen, Pepper thought. There was a massive fireplace and some beautiful rosewood occasional tables. And the books were all leatherbound and old.

Steven ignored these anomalies. 'What is my day looking like, Val?'

The perfect secretary called a page up on the screen without so much as glancing at them. That woman doesn't like me, thought Pepper. She put up her chin. Tough!

The woman ran off a list of appointments. It sounded as if Steven Konig ran the country. What was worse, the subject of each meeting was completely incomprehensible to Pepper.

I've fallen in love with a genius, she thought, depressed. Oh, great. Just what I need. An A-list brain with hormone enhancements.

She had no time to think about it. Steven was saying, 'Lunch?'

'The Dean again.'

'Blow the Dean away,' he said. 'Tell him sorry, but this is a once in a lifetime day.'

Pepper's spine did that zap-to-attention thing again. She thought, I don't believe he said that. A once in a lifetime day? No man has ever thought he would have a once in a lifetime experience with me. It has to be some obscure British joke. This sort of thing just doesn't happen to me.

But Steven was looking across the untidy office straight into Pepper's eyes. His eyes were eager. Surely that couldn't be a joke?

'How do you feel about that?'

He sounded uncertain suddenly. Pepper felt her knees buckle.

'Come on the river with me?' he said softly. 'I'll even read to you.'

So that answered the seduction question. She knew exactly what he was asking. No one had ever asked her like that before, right out in front of other people, speaking a private language that was meant for her ears alone. Her blood drummed.

The perfect secretary seemed unaware of the tension. How could she miss it? thought Pepper. It was there in the room, as strong as the smell of coffee or the sound of thunder.

But the perfect secretary was saying disapprovingly, 'When will you be back, Master?'

'No idea.' He didn't take his eyes off Pepper.

Her thoughts scurried. I don't do this sort of thing, she thought. I feel beautiful. How can he make me feel beautiful just by looking at me? I know I'm not beautiful. But when he looks at me like that...

'And what about Windflower?' said the perfect secretary, oblivious.

'Windflower has a sleepover, thank God.'

He was talking to Val but he did not take his eyes off Pepper. Then his mouth moved, as if he was kissing her skin, and normal service blew apart in a surge of pure lust. Pepper felt herself go hot, cold, then hot again. A voice in her head said, This could be dangerous to your health. To say nothing of your sanity. But this was not a day for listening to voices in her head.

Steven said, 'If I walk you to the covered market, can you pick up a picnic for us?'

Pepper nodded.

'I'll bring the wine.' His smile widened suddenly. 'And the reading matter.'

Libidinous literature? Help!

Pepper could not help herself. She blushed to her eyebrows.

Steven beamed.

CHAPTER SIX

HE WALKED her through the centre of town at top speed, pointing out landmarks as he went.

'Regency terrace. Tudor church. Medieval college. Best bookshop in the world. Biggest salt cellar in the world masquerading as a library.'

Pretty soon Pepper was breathless and her eyes began to pulse. 'Look,' she said, 'I was never designed for competitive walking. And my brain is going into overload here. Please can we stop? That way I can breathe and you can tell me what on earth you're talking about? Salt cellar?'

He didn't actually stop, but he did take her elbow and walk her through a dark arch out into the sun. Then he stopped.

'The Radcliffe Camera,' he said, bowing towards a domed and columned building.

Pepper gasped. It was one of the loveliest buildings she had ever seen. The dome glinted in the sun, atop toast-and-honey brick and slender Doric columns.

'It looks like a classical temple set on top of a bread oven,' she said involuntarily.

Steven chuckled. 'Yup.' He slid his arm round her and drew her close against him. She was sure she could feel his heart beating against her shoulderblade, although he was wearing a jacket, shirt and tie now. Why did he feel so *hot*? 'Like it?' he said, and she thought she could feel his mouth against her hair.

That had to be crazy. Hair had no nerves. It couldn't feel.

Concentrate on what's in front of you, Pepper, never mind the heat-seeking missile to your left; you don't know how to handle it. Think about architecture. You can do this.

The building was certainly worth thinking about. It was

set on a lawn in an open square and flanked by more of those honey-coloured walls. The perspective somehow made it seem smaller than it obviously was.

'Love it,' she said, with all the more enthusiasm because she was trying to ignore the way that every time he breathed in he seemed to pull her closer. 'Do they leave the bicycles there so you know how big it really is?'

'No, the bicycles come with the job description. It's a reading room, mainly for undergraduates. Not science, sadly. I go in there sometimes, just to look at the ceiling of the dome. Better than a cathedral—especially with the sun on it. Lots of gold.'

He released her and looked at his watch. He did not seem as if their closeness had affected him at all. Oh, God, it was that amateur imagination of hers going into overdrive because an attractive man touched her?

I'm pathetic, thought Pepper, furious with herself. I ought to be stamped with a health warning: *This woman can seriously misinterpret your actions.*

'Time to move along, if you're not going to miss your meetings. This way…'

The covered market was a Victorian structure, with wide avenues, high rafters and lots of ironwork. There were dozens of small booths. They seemed to be selling everything from tee shirts to fine wines. The wide aisles smelled of coffee, cheese and leather books.

'Put together in the eighteenth century originally,' said Steven, still in tourist guide mode. 'You might call it the first shopping mall.'

'I'm impressed.'

She meant by his knowledge, but he misunderstood. 'Oh, it's pretty variable. There's quite a bit of tat here. But some nice bookstalls as well. And the food is the best in Oxford. Buy whatever you like for the picnic. I don't eat rollmops, but otherwise I'm an omnivore.'

'I'll remember that,' she said dryly.

He grinned. 'I hope you'll remember a lot more than that. I'll see you at the Camera at noon.'

He bent his tall head and kissed her cheerfully on the cheek. As if he had been doing it all his life. As if they were a couple. Then he was off, briefcase under his arm, whistling.

Pepper stood stock still and tired to get her breath back. *As if they were a couple.* It almost felt as if they were.

Or was that just her lack of experience showing again? Did Steven feel it, too? Or did he drop light kisses on the face of every woman he left to shop?

All too probably, she told herself. Try and keep a hold on reality, Pepper!

She rushed through her meetings. Oh, she made practical notes on the properties on offer. But she couldn't wait to get back to the market, like a child going to its first party.

Steven was right: the food was brilliant. She bought crusty bread that smelled of the oven and was still warm; a collection of morsels from the delicatessen that looked like jewels and gleamed with olive oil and herbs; a great slab of local cheese that the shopkeeper made her try which filled her mouth with the firelight taste of walnuts; grapes; salad; and a great bag of cherries. It was going to be the best picnic of her life!

And then she thought— But I look all wrong.

She was wearing one of her trademark sober business suits. Fine for visiting the Master of an Oxford college. Just right for meeting with potential landlords. Absolute pits for a relaxed picnic on the river. Especially, thought Pepper, with a wicked tilt to her lips, if seduction was on the programme of attractions.

Well, the market had everything. She would just have to buy something more appropriate.

She ended up with a turquoise ruffled skirt, a strappy top bearing the message 'Go for it' picked out in sequins, and a pair of daisy-scattered beach pumps. The whole outfit cost less than one of her usual elegant shirts. Pepper shot gleefully into the ladies' room and changed clothes faster than she had ever changed in her life.

She rolled up her shirt and business suit into a bundle. Catching sight of herself in the mirror, she realised that was exactly what Izzy had done with her party finery last night. In fact, there was not so much difference between them right at this moment. Well, Pepper wasn't fashionably slender, and her underwear was not eye-hurting lime-green. But for once you could tell they were cousins. And not just from the fiery hair.

Quite deliberately, Pepper took what Izzy called a mirror moment. She had left her hair loose this morning—but surely when she'd left home it had not been that riotous cloud of electricity? It looked as if each curl and frond was soaked in sunlight, so that it was shot through with every colour of red from auburn to blood-crimson.

And it was not just her hair. Her brown eyes looked wide and excited. Her mouth was voluptuously full, part-passionate, part-vulnerable. Pepper put up her fingers to her mouth in wonder. And wholly enticing. Oh, yes, she looked like the cousins all right. Seek and seduce with a vengeance!

Emerging again, she paused, her grin fading.

Okay, so seduction was on the programme of attractions. Steven seemed to think so—unless she was getting everything wrong. And now she seemed to be signing up to it, too.

So I'd better be responsible about this, thought Pepper, sobered. All her previous romantic encounters had been with careful sons of her grandmother's acquaintance. In that world men took unspoken charge of the practicalities. They would be affronted if you suggested anything else.

But this was Britain. This was Izzy's and Jemima's country. Pepper had already seen that they did things differently here.

Okay, this was uncharted territory for Pepper. She did not know what Steven would expect of her. But she had lived long enough with her cousins to observe some of the local habits.

She tried to think what Izzy would do. One conclusion was obvious. Pepper made one last stop before she finished her shopping.

'Another first,' she said, soberly pleased with herself. She stuffed the packet of condoms into her handbag and headed for their meeting place.

He proved to be expert on the river. The water around the boathouse was full of punts shunting backwards and forwards, bumping into each other and the bank. Steven, however, sent their boat snaking through the melee without incident. Once clear of the throng, he streaked them up the river, away from all the other boats.

Pepper lay back among cushions and watched the powerful economy of his punting. She remembered what she had thought when she first saw him this morning, all tanned thigh muscles and sexily ruffled hair. She smiled.

'*Do* you work out?'

Steven grinned. 'You say all the right things.'

Pepper chuckled. 'Customer satisfaction is the object at all times. So how often do you go to the gym?'

He shook his head. 'No gym. I run most mornings. And I try to go to the Budokwai once a week.'

'Sounds serious. What do you do at the Budo-thing?'

'Budokwai.' He spelt it out. 'Judo. Done it all my life. It's very balancing.'

She cocked her head to one side. 'I thought it was about kicking the hell out of each other.'

'Not judo. Judo is about managing the prevailing forces. You're supposed to turn your opponent's own strength against him.'

'Pretty sneaky.'

'But a great training for life.'

There was a smile in his eyes. Pepper lounged at his feet, looking up at him, and that look in his eyes was like a kiss.

More than a kiss. She stretched luxuriantly and watched his eyes flicker.

Yes! she thought, exultant.

Eventually they came to a quiet stretch of river and Steven slid the punt in to the bank under the shimmering curtain of a willow tree. He drove the punt pole into the riverbed, constricting the punt's movement.

Eventually the boat's gentle rocking faded to nothing. The long willow fronds swayed and then, slowly, returned to perfect stillness. In the afternoon heat nothing moved, except water boatmen darting over the dark, diamond-flecked water. Even the birds were silent.

Steven lay down beside Pepper.

She tensed. Oh, Lord, here it comes. The full seduction by summer. I know I thought I'd signed up to it. But now it's here, I'm not sure. It's been too long… I wish I were twenty pounds lighter… I wish I knew more about him… I could get into very deep water here… *Help!*

She held her breath until she shook with the effort of it. But all Steven did was put his hands behind his head and look up through the willow.

'I'd breathe soon if I were you,' he said, still staring upwards. 'Or you'll pass out.' His voice took on an edge. 'And then you don't know what I might do.'

Pepper gave a great explosive gasp and the boat rocked. She grabbed for the side and sat up, glaring at him.

'What?'

He still did not look at her. 'All you have to do is say no, you know,' he said in a conversational tone.

Pepper ground her teeth. 'What do you mean?'

'What I say. You haven't made up your mind yet.' He withdrew his eyes from the sky briefly and gave her a long, level look. 'I can live with that. I'd rather not have you lying there palpitating, though. I'm not about to ravish you against your will.'

Ouch!

After a moment Pepper said in a suffocated voice, 'Am I so transparent?'

He softened. 'Hey, we're both on a learning curve here.'

'I'm sorry.' She was really perturbed.

'No sweat. We'll work it out. For now, why don't you just kick back and drink in the day?'

Slowly, awkwardly, she lay down again. Her limbs felt as stiff as a china doll's. But Steven did not make a move towards her and eventually she followed his eyes, up through the willow.

The sun was spraying tiny rainbows off thousands of leaves. It was like lying in the heart of a waterfall. She closed her eyes, dazzled. Her breathing steadied a little.

'Perfect,' she heard him say dreamily.

Eyes still shut, Pepper felt her hand taken. Held gently, but very firmly. And slowly, slowly, the tension went out of her. Her head quietened. And her heart—her heart began to open. Open to the sun; to murmurous not-quite-silence; to the man who would not ravish her against her will. Who was on a learning curve, too.

Who was holding her hand as if they belonged together. And who wasn't going to do anything else until she made up her mind...

Pepper made up her mind. 'Steven,' she said softly.

'Yes?'

'Hold me?'

There was a moment when everything seemed suspended. A bit of Pepper was crouching inside her head with its hands over its eyes moaning, I can't believe you just said that. But all the rest of her was waiting when Steven came up on his elbow, rather carefully, and bent over her.

It was a long, surprising embrace. Pepper began to realise just how little she had discovered about her own desires in all her previous experience.

Experience? Huh! This was experience. Everything else before today had been sex by numbers. She realised that now. You followed the guidelines and you got pleasure. Steven could make her feel more with a fingertip to her parted lips than she had ever felt in her life before.

Feel more? Who was she kidding. He made her *want* more! Want as she had never wanted before. And all without once losing his own immaculate control. Not even when she heard herself cry out in amazed delight.

Oh, wow, am I into uncharted territory here.

Burying her face in the curve of his shoulder, she clung to him. Slowly the convulsive trembling stilled. Slowly her pulses returned to normal. Delight remained, though. Delight in every atom of her body.

Eventually Pepper stirred. 'Kissing girls in a punt has to be a specialised skill,' she said. 'And, boy, have you got it!'

Steven raised his head. 'Why, thank you, ma'am.'

She held herself away from him, dazed and trying not to show it. 'Put in a lot of practice?'

His arms tightened. 'I could use some more.'

Pepper searched his face. His kiss had left her tingling to her toes. But he seemed unmoved. Well, not unmoved exactly. Just not carried away.

As if to underline Steven's continued equilibrium, the punt swayed as serenely as a rocking chair. Steven's expression was a potent mixture of laughter, pleasure and anticipation. All shared.

Not dazed, though. She didn't send him into orbit the way he sent her. Pepper Calhoun, come in. Your time is up!

Regretfully, she sat up and tried to find her docking station on Planet Earth.

'Hey, what about this picnic I brought? My self-esteem will be zero if we don't eat.'

He did not try to pull her back into his arms. Nor did he try to argue back. Surely he would have argued if he had been the smallest, tiniest bit dazed?

But he didn't. Instead he said, 'And there's champagne, too.'

Pepper looked at him cautiously. 'Is this a celebration?'

Steven's eyes crinkled wickedly. 'Purely practical. I don't carry a corkscrew. With champagne you don't need one.'

She gave up and served the food.

He approved her choice, savoured the olives, raved about the cheese. He also plied her with a lovely creamy, biscuity champagne from a coolbag and put her through the third degree. Sitting cross-legged opposite her, he dragged stuff out of her she had not even told her cousins.

'So what happened to the feud?'

Pepper spilt some of her third glass. 'What?'

'The first time we met you said you were going to try to make peace in a family feud.'

She was surprised. 'You remember that?'

He toasted her silently. 'I remember everything you ever said to me.'

'Even when you were so vile to me at Indigo?'

He had the grace to look ashamed. 'It was a bad day for me. And then you started throwing your weight about and it seemed as if you were the worst sort of aggressive woman. I think I was so nasty because I felt a fool.'

'A fool?' She didn't understand.

'I told you,' Steven said levelly. 'I remember everything you've ever said to me. On the plane you were—wonderful.'

Their eyes met. All of a sudden Pepper was breathless. Maybe he was a little bit dazed after all, then.

He leaned towards her.

A great wave of confusion washed over. She looked away, straightening, swallowing. It was the tiniest recoil. Her body moved a few millimetres, that was all.

But Steven stopped as if he had been shot.

There was silence. Fool, fool, *fool*, yelled Pepper's inner commentator. But she could not think of a thing to say.

And then Steven was saying easily, 'So, tell me about the feud.'

She was grateful for the lifeline. And disappointed that she needed it. She paddled back into shallow waters and tried to concentrate.

She drummed up a smile from somewhere. 'Peace made. In fact, I'm rooming with my cousins.' She smiled more easily at the thought. 'They're great. A real education.'

Steven replaced her spilt champagne. 'How so?'

'I've never done girl-talk before,' Pepper said seriously. 'Ask me about a P/E ratio and I'm fine. But all that sitting round rapping at midnight—hell, no.'

He was bewildered. 'Sorry—not with you.'

She grinned. 'How to be hot. How to be cool. How to say more than you mean. And how to find the ES.'

Steven blinked. 'I'm lost. What's the ES?'

Pepper bubbled over. 'Endangered Species. The single, straight, solvent male.'

His eyes danced suddenly. 'Now, there I'm with you. And you can stop looking.'

All desire to laugh left her. 'What?' she said uncertainly.

He took her hand. His grip was very strong and his hand was hot. She scanned his face. There was a faint colour along his cheekbones and his breath was definitely coming faster. It wasn't exactly the pirate back, but there was more than a hint of recklessness in his dark eyes.

Maybe this was better than dazed, thought Pepper in confusion. Was it her imagination, or could she feel his blood pulsing through in time to her own?

'Only area of debate is my solvency,' he murmured provocatively. 'Come back to my place and I'll show you my portfolio.'

It hung in the air, half a joke, half a step further on the road. A road she wanted to travel. Didn't she?

Pepper gulped. This was the sort of sexy teasing that she knew Izzy and Jemima relished. She knew you were supposed to tease right back. Only she could not think of a thing to say.

She froze, and sat there, wretched at her own incompetence.

Steven Konig seemed to forgive her. More, he seemed to understand. He touched her face very gently, like a promise.

'Time to read to you, perhaps?'

Was this where he read her some wildly sexy love poetry? Would that make it easier to take that crucial next step? Pepper found she was torn between excitement and acute embarrassment. But the book he produced was a paperback and she knew the title.

'The Wind in the Willows?' she said incredulously.

'You said you loved it,' he said simply. 'And this is supposed to be a perfect day.'

If he had still been holding her hand she would have responded to him then. Without thought, without reserve.

But he wasn't holding her hand any more. Or even looking at her. He was opening the book and resting it against his bended knees.

'Now, listen,' he said, and began to read from the book.

It was, indeed, a perfect day.

He read to her. And then they talked. Then they lay peacefully side by side, watching the play of light on water, not saying anything. The shadows lengthened and the birds began to wake up. A little breeze arose. Pepper shivered in her market-bought top. But she did not want to leave the shelter of the willow curtain.

'We should go,' said Steven.

Everything in Pepper screamed, *No! Not yet!*

But he did not move. It was as if he, too, did not want to venture out from their enchanted hiding place.

Not looking at her, he said, 'Want to come back and see the college properly?'

Pepper was hugely relieved. 'Sure.'

She had no idea what time it was, but the evening was certainly gathering in. She had a day return ticket on the train. But she did not even ask about the timetable of the last train to London. Somehow she felt that the day had a natural rhythm and it would be bad luck not to go with the flow.

Well, that was what she told herself. In her heart of hearts she admitted that she just wanted to be with Steven Konig for as long as she could get. She had never wanted to be with anyone like that before. Usually she could not wait to get back to the project of the moment. To her real life, as she thought of it. Only now this felt like the only thing in her life that was real.

They took the punt back to the boathouse. It was even busier than it had been in the afternoon.

'We could eat here, if you wanted?' Steven nodded at tables under the trees. 'Or a drink?'

Pepper shook her head. 'Not hungry.'

Well, she was. But not for food or warm English beer.

She packed up the remains of the picnic and the bag containing her business suit as he pulled the punt into its mooring with expert precision. He handed her out of the boat.

'Careful,' said Pepper, wobbling a bit as she put a foot to dry land, 'you don't want the elephant to drag you into the water. I can be a real klutz.'

He looked at her frowningly. But an attendant came up to take the cushions from their punt and Steven had to take time out to pay him.

When that was done he turned to her and said, 'Are you seriously calling yourself an elephant?'

Pepper flung up a hand. 'Don't let's talk about my failings,' she said dryly. 'It's been such a lovely day.'

His frown deepened.

But she said, 'Please?' and he gave in, though he continued to look disturbed.

'Walk back? Or I can call a taxi? Or we can ride part of the way on the bus. Very ethnic.'

Pepper voted for walking. 'You said it, after all. Food in, energy out. Exercise is exactly what I need.'

Steven stopped dead. 'Will you please stop putting yourself down?' he said furiously. 'I'll walk to the North Pole with you if you like. But no more insulting yourself, please.'

'Okay,' said Pepper, taken aback. She moved slightly away from him, clasping her arms about herself. As always, when she felt criticised, she heard her voice turn frosty. 'You've got it.'

'I didn't mean—*hell*!' His eyes sharpened. 'You're cold. We are certainly not walking back if you're cold. Here, take this.'

He had been carrying the jacket of his business suit over his arm. Now he stopped and swung it round her shoulders.

He took her back to the college. There were a lot more students than there had been this morning. They stood around, in the porter's lodge and chatting outside in the sunshine. It must be her guilty conscience that made her feel that they were all looking at her, Pepper thought.

Or, if not conscience, then her tee shirt and turquoise skirt, she thought wryly. They could not be used to seeing their Master escorting a woman who looked so—well—unbuttoned. Between the slogan in sequins and the willow seeds in her tangled hair, she felt younger and more unserious than she had ever felt in her life before. She quite liked the sensation. But it made her feel uneasy all the same.

'I'm letting you down,' she muttered, embarrassed.

He snorted. 'You have no idea how much you're boosting my image. Now—the full guided tour.'

He took her everywhere, ending with a flourish in the main quadrangle, overlooked by late medieval brickwork. 'Welcome to Queen Margaret's College,' he said formally.

Pepper was silent for a moment. She felt humbled. She had been to some of the most distinguished seats of learning in the world, one way and another, but for sheer beauty she had never seen anything to rival Queen Margaret's. She felt even more out of place in her tawdry cotton and sequins, but Steven looked as if he'd been born there.

'Very impressive,' she said slowly. 'I've seen story books with Gothic illustrations like this.' Her gesture included the whole quad.

'Yes,' said Steven depressed. 'It's pure fairy tale. And the roof leaks.'

She was startled into a spurt of laughter. 'What?'

'Gothic building is a lot more picturesque than solid. The upkeep is ruinous.'

Pepper bent her powerful financial brain to the problem and perceived a flaw. 'But surely you must have endowments? Benefactors?'

'No, that's what we *need*.' He made a face at an ill-tempered gargoyle just below the roofline. After a brief hesitation, he added casually, 'Actually, that's why they wanted me as Master in the first place. I'm not your traditional head of college, by any means.'

Pepper looked at him. He had removed his jacket and tie, but his shirt had withstood the oily boat and the shedding willow better than her tee shirt. And it was not just a matter of dress. Steven Konig had that indefinable air of contained power, as if he had thought through all the big problems of life and knew where he stood on every one of them. He made the men she had known before, men like Ed Ivanov, look like boys.

She said tartly, 'What do they want, Methuselah?'

He gave a startled laugh. 'Maybe. If he had a family trust wanting to invest in education.'

He was laughing, but somehow Pepper knew that this was a sore point.

'Explain.'

But he shook his head, shrugging. 'Dull stuff to end a perfect day. Let me take you to the buttery and buy you a beer. Now, that's something that your average tourist would miss. Very ethnic.'

Pepper laughed and let him walk her round the quad to the chapel door. But she said, 'I'd still like to know why a college this old is short of funds.'

Steven gave a crack of laughter. He opened the heavy oak door for her. 'Our history: we were set up out of pique by a woman who wanted to prove she cared about learning just as much as her husband did.'

Their steps echoed on the old flags of the chapel. It was smaller and plainer than was expected. She said so.

'Quite. The college was a five-day wonder with Queen Margaret. She got bored and never got around to paying up the second instalment. Come along. Library next.'

They went out into the summer evening again.

'But surely, after all these centuries...'

'We've never been a grand college,' said Steven. 'Small tends to mean poor, you know. All through the eighteenth century, when every other college's pupils were making their fortune, we turned out dull clerics. No Indian nabobs.'

Pepper was entertained. 'And since?'

He pulled a comical face. 'Same old story. No Prime Ministers. No pop moguls. Every college in Oxford is on the fund-raising trail these days. Queen Margaret's starts right at the back of the field. And I'm turning out to be rubbish.'

He smiled, but she could see that it really bugged him.

She slid her arm through his. 'Maybe we should talk about this. I've never actually been a fund-raiser, but we covered it in business school. And I got the prize for problem solving.'

He squeezed her hand. 'Then we must definitely talk about it.'

He walked her through the library, a simple eighteenth century room full of beautiful wood and bulging bookshelves. 'Needs an extension,' said Steven. 'And rewiring. We'll skip the dining hall. They will still be at dinner. But you'll like the buttery.'

The buttery turned out to be a vaulted cellar, with a wooden floor and rough tables, full of students and the smell of fast food.

'Hi there, Kong,' said one who was acting as barman. He gave Steven a high five and called out to a group at the end of the room, 'Hey, Francis, Geoff—it's the King.'

Most people looked up, but nobody got too excited about their Master appearing in their beer cellar, thought Pepper. They accepted her presence without much interest, too. The little knot at the end of the room turned out to have been standing round a dartboard. They challenged Steven to a dart match.

'And your guest, too, of course.'

'Ms Calhoun,' Steven said, introducing her meticulously, and to Pepper, 'Do you play darts?'

'I had a bow and arrow when I was child,' she said doubtfully.

'That'll do. Two against two, Geoff, okay? The usual stakes.'

By the end of the match she was hitting the dartboard with sixty per cent of her throws.

'They like you, don't they?' she murmured, as he sat down after throwing three darts rather badly.

Steven was unmoved. 'That's because I always lose.' His eyes glinted. 'Even when you aren't here to support me.'

She put her nose in the air. 'That's cheating.'

'No, it's not. It's a way of buying a round without anyone feeling patronised.'

Pepper was puzzled.

'I was a student here. I remember when it was a choice between a pint or a paperback,' he said with feeling. 'And I like it in here. Makes a really nice change from the senior common room.'

'What have you got against the senior common room?' she teased.

Steven looked irritated. 'Ask rather what they've got against me. Some of them don't like it when I accept television invitations like the Indigo thing. It's supposed to be part of my job to keep the college in the public eye. But the Dean and his party think it makes me a media junkie. Which is just another thing to put on the charge sheet. Along with setting off fireworks on the tower when I was nineteen and not being a proper academic.'

Before she could answer he was called back to the dartboard. He went.

She studied him. He took his time to measure the distance.

Then threw. Clearly he brought the same concentration to the bar room game as he did to everything else.

Care and precision, thought Pepper. That was what Steven Konig applied to everything. Darts. Entrepreneurship. Kissing girls in punts.

Making love?

She gave a little shiver of pure lust at the thought.

He threw a score which was high enough to be respectable, low enough to get him beaten. Just as he'd said he would.

'You're good, aren't you?' she said as he resumed his seat beside her.

He looked straight into her eyes and said with total innocence, 'My co-ordination has always been much admired.'

Pepper did not blink. 'You're trying to make me blush and you're not going to,' she told him calmly. 'Tell me why you're not a proper academic.'

Steven shrugged. 'I'm not a brilliant original scientist. Kplant isn't at the cutting edge of research. What I do brilliantly is put together isolated bits of research and see what the implications are.'

Pepper thought about it. 'But don't lots of people do that sort of thing?'

'No. Scientists are awful snobs. And so narrow. No decent research scientist will stray outside his own field. And simple businessmen won't understand the basic science. So I've pretty much got the field to myself.' He pulled a face. 'That's how I got my short-lived Professor's Chair. And why I do about twenty jobs at any one time.'

She said slowly, 'I thought you were an entrepreneur.'

'So I was, for a bit. Now I'm just non-executive Chair of my own company. Or at least I am until I've finished my tour of duty here. But originally I was a chemist.' He pulled a face. 'Sorry! Boring or what?'

'No,' said Pepper. She wanted to touch him so much that she thought she must look as if she were on fire. And he thought he was *boring*?

He grinned. 'There's no need to be kind. I'm under no

illusion. I always was pretty boring. And when I first started to find a way to synthesise nutrients with texture, I was a real social liability.' His eyes lit with reminiscent amusement. 'Courtney once told me that I talked through two courses in formal hall without drawing breath or noticing that I hadn't eaten anything. She was not pleased at the time.'

For a moment Pepper flinched. Who was Courtney?

She longed to ask. She didn't dare to ask. She had no right to ask.

She said instead, 'Is that what you always wanted to do?'

'Make synthetic food?' Steven looked at her as if she were crazy. 'I don't think any adolescent boy dreams of stuff like that. I wanted to go to the moon. Or save the world, maybe.'

'So how did you fall into synthetic food?'

'I was good at chemistry.' He leaned back in the oak settle, looking round the cheerful bar, smiling reminiscently. 'I made terrific explosions. It was a great social asset.'

'What?'

He put his hands behind his head. 'I was a bit of a refugee when it came to schoolwork. I loved it. But I came from a high-rise, where every other boy my age was into football violence and hanging round the town centre. The nearest they got to an interest in science was stealing spare parts from cars. Only child, too. I was a real outsider.'

Pepper shook her head. 'I can't imagine it,' she said, humbled. 'It must have been just awful.'

He looked surprised. 'It had its moments. The guys who were my more natural peers all lived on the other side of town in nice suburbs, with books and two parents. And, of course, they were suspicious about this tough from the war zone. But I learned their language and I could always do those spectacular explosions in old dog food tins. I was a real crowd-pleaser on Bonfire Night. In the end they accepted me. In fact my friend Tom's parents virtually adopted me when my dad died.' His smile grew sad. 'In fact Tom was the reason I chose Maggie's.'

'Maggie's?'

'Queen Margaret's College, God bless it. Tom's dad had been here. So we both applied. And got in.' He looked round the bar again. 'We used to drink in here when we were these guys' age.' His expression hardened. 'And those idiots in the senior common room think I don't *care* about the college. Who else would do what I do? I may not be academically respectable, but by God they need me.'

'Do you want to be academically respectable?' Pepper asked thoughtfully.

Steven shifted his shoulders. 'We all want respect,' he said evasively.

Pepper looked at him sharply. He sounded defeated. Pepper could hardly believe it. Masterful, witty, responsible Steven Konig—*defeated*? She felt suddenly fiercely angry with the Dean and the academic snobs.

'You definitely need a prize-winning problem solver,' she said. 'Count me in.'

He went very still for a moment. Then he said in an odd voice, 'Are you feeling *sorry* for me, Pepper?'

Oh, heavens, she thought. Big mistake! What was it Izzy had said? The biggest turn-off in the world was to make a guy feel he couldn't cope?

'I didn't mean that. I mean, not the way it sounded. I meant…'

He touched her cheek. 'Oh, sweetheart,' he said, with such a wealth of tenderness in his voice that she shuddered to a halt, blinking.

'Just voting myself onto the team,' she said in a small voice.

'*My* team,' he said quietly.

And raised her hand to his lips.

Pepper quivered and was still. They sat and looked into each other's eyes in perfect silence.

He stirred. 'I'd better go and get that round in.' He stood up, but held onto her hand as if he could not bear to let it go. Then he brushed his mouth over her knuckles again. 'Don't go away. I've got a rose garden to show you.'

CHAPTER SEVEN

THE garden was a wilderness of blousy blooms, all tangled and riotously out of control. They filled the night air with voluptuous scent. Pepper stopped dead and drew the honeyed air into her lungs. She felt as if she were floating on her awakened senses.

'This is just amazing.'

Steven hugged her against his side. 'This is the result of staff cuts,' he said ruefully. 'We can only afford a part-time gardener, and he spends most of his time nursing the lawn in the main quad. The roses just do their own thing.'

'They've got the right idea,' said Pepper with enthusiasm. She stuffed her nose in some great cabbagey thing that smelt of warm lemons and murmured appreciatively.

'You're not an expensive date, are you?' said Steven, touched.

'I'm discriminating,' she corrected with dignity.

His arm tightened. 'You are indeed.'

They wandered along overgrown paths until the sky was completely dark. There were no clouds and a thin sickle moon incised a sharp little curve into a dusting of stars.

'Oh, isn't it lovely? And so wonderful that it's just us,' said Pepper, letting her head fall dreamily onto Steven's shoulder. 'Is everyone else being tactful?'

'It's the Master's Garden. Everyone else only gets to come here if I invite them. I took the precaution of locking the garden gate when we got back,' said Steven smugly.

'Forethought,' approved Pepper. Between the night and the smell of roses and her own secret fantasies she was feeling slightly high. 'Impressive.'

'Thank you. So, now you've done the Master's Garden, do you want to inspect the Master's Lodging?'

Somewhere deep inside Pepper something began to quiver. 'I thought I saw it this morning.'

'There's more to the Master's Lodging than a heritage staircase and a dodgy kitchen.'

'I-Is there?'

'Want to see?' he murmured.

Yes. No. I don't know. *Help!*

'Yes,' she said, so loudly that they both jumped.

His arm was suddenly a vice, nearly crushing her ribs. If it hadn't been crazy, she would have said Steven was shaking, too.

'Good.' He led her to a small door in the side of the curved wall. A forest of scented blooms climbed over it but neither of them paused to savour the perfume. He produced a heavy iron key from his pocket and flung open the door with a flourish. 'My house is your house.'

Pepper went inside. She followed him upstairs to his untidy sitting room and looked round. Stone walls, flagstones, oak panelling. Books everywhere. It looked like a magician's den in a secret castle.

Oh, wow, she thought. Bring on the candlelight and log fires, we're in for a Traditional English Seduction. Can I deal with this?

She cleared her throat. Loudly. 'I feel outclassed,' she announced. It came out a lot more aggressive than she meant. It almost sounded like a challenge.

Steven took it calmly, though. He touched her cheek briefly. 'You're not outclassed, sweetheart. You're the most spectacular thing these old walls have seen in a long time.'

'Spectacular!' She was stunned.

Steven's smile tilted ruefully. 'You'd better believe it.'

Pepper shook her head, unable to believe it. 'Wearing a vulgar tee shirt and leaves in my hair?'

He laughed aloud. 'Not just leaves.'

He reached out and picked something off her head, then held his hand out to her.

She looked at his palm. 'Rose petals?'

'Very romantic,' said Steven with a straight face. 'Goes well with the pollen on your nose.'

Pepper jumped. 'I haven't,' she said automatically.

'Look.'

He nodded towards an alcove and Pepper realised that there was an old mirror on the wall. It had a gilded baroque frame and a badly spotted surface. But it reflected a face back at her that bore all the grubbiness of a day in the meadow and an evening among cobwebby roses. Pepper licked a finger and ran it down her cheek. The result was a clear dust trail. She groaned.

'What a mess I am.'

'You're enchanting,' Steven said huskily.

She shifted focus and saw that he was watching her in the spotty old mirror. Her eyes widened. *He wants me*, she thought. For the first time in her life she had no doubts about that at all.

He touched her shoulder almost tentatively.

Suddenly, blindingly, her body remembered her instant response to him on the plane. He had only had to touch her and the turbulence had started. It was the same now. Maybe it was because he was touching her. Maybe it was because it was so late that the shadowy beard was beginning to appear again and she remembered that raffish, dangerous look.

Or maybe it was neither. Maybe it was the look in his eyes. In the mirror, it was somehow naked.

Oh, yes, he wanted her all right. *And I want him.*

Pepper stood straighter. She felt as if she had come to a point of no return: scared and yet somehow very calm.

Steven said quietly, 'I want you to stay.'

'I know.' She sounded very grown-up, thought Pepper, amazed. Inside she had never felt less grown-up in her life. Inside her thoughts were motoring frantically: *I can deal with this. I have got to deal with this. Or spend the rest of my life wishing I had.* But outwardly she was totally composed.

Into her silence he said, 'I know we haven't spent a lot of time together. All I can say is—I feel as if I've always known you.'

Pepper drew a deep breath. She turned to face him.

'Will you stay?' It was oddly formal, almost like a vow.

She swallowed. 'Yes.'

He took her by the hand and led her up the spiral staircase. Pepper went, outwardly assured, inwardly quaking.

She wanted to make love with Steven. Of course she did. Heck, if he opened her purse he'd find the evidence that she'd even planned for it.

All through this afternoon, under the golden willow, she had hardly been able to keep her hands off him. But now that it was going to happen—her mouth dried.

Will I remember what to do? Oh, I still know what goes where, but what about all those secret little signs that people make? Oh, why didn't I talk to Izzy properly this morning? Why did I just stick my nose in the air and say I wasn't a virgin? As if that was all there was to worry about!

And what on earth do you say?

As if he could hear her thoughts, Steven tightened his fingers round hers.

'We'll be all right,' he said over his shoulder.

For a moment Pepper almost dragged her hand away. *Does he feel sorry for me?* she thought, appalled.

But then he said, 'Staircases are always a risk,' and she relaxed.

Well, a little. She didn't pull her hand away, anyway.

'What do you mean?'

'I bet more people have changed their mind on the stairs than anywhere else.' He stopped and swung round. 'Is this where you usually have second thoughts? Are you having them now?'

Pepper bit her lip, not answering.

'Oh, God, you are. I've messed this up, haven't I?'

Pepper searched his face. He looked desperately earnest. Not the laughing seducer any more. Just a man as confused as she was.

'I should have carried you,' he castigated himself. 'That's the only way to do it, isn't it?'

She thought, I could hurt this man badly.

Aloud she said, 'Carrying me would be a real passion-killer.'

He was even more confused. 'What?'

'That little exercise problem we were talking about earlier, remember? I'm not a size to be carried. I like my men standing,' said Pepper dryly. She went up a step. The staircase was so narrow that she had to crowd on the tread beside him. Their bodies touched everywhere.

Steven groaned, his eyes closing involuntarily.

Pepper held his head to receive her kiss. 'Besides,' she said huskily, 'this has compensations.'

And moved.

She never remembered afterwards how they got up the rest of the staircase. She only knew that she stopped worrying about what she was supposed to say.

Or do, for that matter. Steven left her in no doubt about that. He made love like a man inspired.

At one point Pepper flung herself back on the covers—they had not actually made it *into* bed—and laughed until she choked.

'You're laughing at me?' said Steven. 'I'm hurt.'

As he was kissing her stomach at the time, and showed no signs of being discouraged, Pepper did not take this very seriously.

She ruffled his hair. 'No, you're not. You're wonderful.'

He raised his head at that and looked at her, all the way along her naked and indulged body. His eyes gleamed. 'Why, thank you, ma'am,' he drawled.

She lay among the pillows and blew him a kiss. It was provocative. It was meant to be.

He swung round and hauled himself up on his elbow, leaning over her with a curious expression.

'I bet no woman ever laughed at Captain Blood,' he complained.

Pepper blinked. 'Captain who?'

'Never mind. What were you laughing at? Not my technique, I hope.'

She was shaken by wicked laughter. 'Yes, I was, in a way.'

He caught her wrist as she went to stroke his face and held it pinned above her head.

'Madam, you mock me at your peril,' he growled. 'Which way?'

'I remembered you telling me you were just a boring chemist,' she teased. 'Boring! In your dreams!'

'You inspire me,' he said, mock solemn.

He leaned in closer, touching his mouth to her nose, her cheekbones, her closing eyelids, her mouth.

Her mouth...

Pepper convulsed. She dragged him down to her, beyond talk, beyond laughter, beyond even that golden gentleness that moved her to the edge of tears. Suddenly she could not wait any longer. There was a new road ahead of her. She had to set out *now*.

'Touch me,' she ground out. It was a voice she did not recognise.

The road took her to a place she had not been before. She had not known it was possible to feel so focused, so utterly concentrated.

So powerful.

Or so loved.

They say that after earthquakes, when everything has settled into its new landscape, there is total silence. The thought came to Pepper as, later, they lay satiated and unmoving. Everything felt new, all right, from her brain out. And in that new silence she made a discovery.

I love you, she said to him in her head, as he lay collapsed across her in the aftermath.

But she did not say it aloud. And, as for Steven, he seemed beyond speech.

She did not know how long they lay like that in each other's arms. Eventually Steven got up. Left alone, Pepper came out of her trance. She got up, too, and padded among their scattered clothes, looking for a tee shirt.

She looked around the shadowed room. The bed looked naked. The dark green sheet was wildly creased and coming away from the corner.

'That bed is a wreck,' said Steven complacently.

He came up behind her and clipped her body back against his. She could not believe the warmth of him, the strength of the arm round her. She felt his breath in her hair and realised he was laughing again.

It was not hard to see why.

The bed was indeed a wreck. There were no pillows left on it. The coverlet had slid off into a heap on the floor. The oversheet was a twisted rope in the corner. Pepper remembered—she thought she remembered—kicking it away in a surge of impatience as she writhed about him, reaching to be closer, and ever closer. Or was it Steven who had kicked the sheet off the bed in that final moment of ecstasy?

I don't where he ends and I begin, she thought. It startled her.

He stroked her breast absently. 'Cold?'

'No.'

'I thought you shivered,' he said on a faint note of query.

'No.'

'You all right, sweetheart?'

She put both hands over his protecting arm, hugging him. 'I'm great.'

'Seconded.' His voice was full of tender amusement.

Pepper leaned her head back against his naked shoulder. She could feel his heart under her cheek. It was steady as the pulse of the universe.

She thought, I'm home.

Quite suddenly, she knew without question that she belonged with this man. Pepper was awed. She had never felt that before. Never even imagined feeling it.

It felt as if she had put down a burden she did not know she had been carrying. She was free! She gave a little shiver of amazed delight.

His arms tightened. 'You *are* cold. Wrap yourself in that while I make us a bed fit to sleep on.'

She found an old robe dropped round her shoulders. She sank down onto an oak chest and watched while he straightened the sheet, pounded the pillows back into shape and flung them back into place, unwound the oversheet and restored it and the coverlet.

'Very domestic,' she teased, glowing with love.

He kissed her shoulder as he passed. 'Oh, I'm not just a pretty face.'

'I'm impressed.'

He chuckled. 'Good.'

He worked with swift efficiency. As if he had done exactly this many times before.

Pepper clutched the robe closer.

Careful, she told herself. Of course he has done this before. That has nothing to do with you. But she felt a little colder.

She was spiralling back down to earth and she didn't want to. She watched the bunch and release of muscles in his back as he worked and thought, He is really, really fantastic without his clothes. No wonder Jemima said he was gorgeous. He is.

Gorgeous. And all those other women who have sat here watching him were probably gorgeous, too. She pulled the robe tighter.

It took about a minute to get the bed straight. And to send Pepper into silent terror. By the time Steven got her back into bed her head had managed to detach itself from her hated body and was somewhere on the outer edge of the galaxy and travelling fast.

He did not pick up the widening distance between them,

it seemed. He tucked her competently into the crook of his arm and settled himself down to sleep.

'Comfortable?'

'Very, thank you,' said Pepper politely. She was lying in her teeth.

He did not realise that either. 'Good.'

She felt him fall asleep beside her. His breathing slowed. Then his sheltering arm slackened and fell away.

Pepper waited a moment and then, very carefully, eased away from him. She was horribly awake. *Comfortable?* How on earth was she supposed to be comfortable? She was a potato, taking up too much room in a strange bed. He would never have taken a potato to bed before. However kind and funny Steven Konig was, there was no way she could get round that.

She was the woman who'd had to have a social life organised by her rich family; the wallflower at the high school prom; the businesswoman without a heart. And the sooner she got back where she belonged the better! Before she started to build too much on Steven Konig's spellbinding courtesy in bed. Or his kindness. If she let herself believe it was more than kindness, she might just end up breaking her heart.

Pepper's eyes ached with staring at the darkness. But she did not cry. She might wake him up if she cried, and she did not think she could bear that. So she kept her mind grimly on track on its outward journey from paradise. By the morning she had reached deep space.

Steven did not realise it. He wandered around the bedroom chatting as if they had woken up together hundreds of times before. His whole manner said, This is no big deal.

I wish I thought it was no big deal, thought Pepper miserably. I wish I knew how to handle this. If only I were more like Izzy and Jemima. I don't even know what to *say*, for heaven's sake.

'Would you get my suit for me, please? I left it in a carrier bag downstairs somewhere.'

Steven pulled a laughing face. 'Spoilsport. I'm going to miss that tee shirt.'

Pepper smiled, but it was an effort. Steven was back in piratical mode again. His dark hair looked as if he had been facing a high wind off the Spanish Main and his jaw was dark with stubble. He did not look courteous and civilised. He looked like raw sexuality incarnate. And way, way out of her league, sequinned tee shirt or no.

She said politely, 'I'd like to be properly dressed when your housekeeper arrives, if you know what I mean.'

Oh, heavens, it sounded so sophisticated. The man had stripped her to the heart last night, and now here she was talking to him as if she were a guest at one of her grandmother's pool parties! Pepper really hated herself in that moment. But she was floundering. She did not seem to be able to do anything about it.

Steven shook his head at her, his dark eyes alight with laughter.

'Time for a reality check. No housekeeper. The college can't afford it.'

'Oh? Then who takes care of—er—' She could not remember the child's real name. All she could remember was that it was *not* Janice.

His eyes stopped laughing. 'Windflower,' he supplied. 'I do.' He looked at her curiously. 'Is that a problem?'

Pepper jumped. 'No, of course not.'

He looked at her searchingly. 'She's not here this morning, you know. She had a sleepover with a friend. You don't have to worry about coming face to face with her over the bacon and eggs.'

Pepper swallowed. This was worse than any of the other morning goodbyes she had said in her time. Why did he have to look like a teen queen's fantasy and yet be so kind?

'No bacon and eggs,' she said in a light, bright voice that, if she were Steven, would have made her want to hit her. *Why am I behaving like this?* But she didn't seem to be able to stop. 'I can do you toast and coffee, but if you want hash browns you're on your own.'

He stopped wandering around the bedroom at that, and looked at her narrow-eyed. She saw the friendliness drain out of him like sand out of an egg-timer.

'I should have thought of that. Rich girls don't cook?'

'I'm not a rich girl any more,' she said crisply.

'No one would guess it,' he retorted. He came up to her and took her by the shoulders. His hands were gentle but the eyes that searched her face were not. 'What's happening here?' he said quietly. 'I went to bed with a voluptuary and woke up with a picky princess.'

A voluptuary! What he meant was desperate. Pepper thought she would die, it hurt so much.

She gabbled, 'Don't bother about the suit. I'll get it myself,' and bolted out of the bedroom.

He caught up with her in the kitchen eventually. She had put coffee on. She had also skewered her tangled hair back into place so hard it made her eyes water. Yesterday's blouse was creased, so she'd put her jacket on to hide the damage.

Steven stood in the doorway and took in the change in her appearance. 'On your way already?' he said dryly.

She avoided his eyes. 'I'm sorry?'

He indicated her be-suited figure with a disparaging gesture. 'So good of you to delay your departure to put the coffee on. Above and beyond the call of duty.'

Pepper kept her smile in place, though it made her jaw ache. To say nothing of her heart. 'My pleasure.'

'Is it?' He took a step forward. 'You don't look as if anything about this is a pleasure. What's wrong, Pepper?'

If he had touched her perhaps she would have let her guard down and all her terrible doubts would have spilled out. Perhaps. But he didn't touch her. He stood looking at her as if he did not know what was happening and she thought, His other women behave differently. It was a killer.

She looked away. 'Nothing's wrong. I just have to get back to work. I took too much time out yesterday.' She gave a little artificial laugh. 'I don't know what happened to me. Yesterday was an aberration.'

He went very still. 'I see.'

Hell! 'I didn't mean that.'

'I think you did.'

'Well, not the way it sounded.' She was floundering, the words falling over themselves. 'I don't sleep with strangers.'

His eyes were intent suddenly. 'And you think I do?'

'I don't know what you do,' she said on a note of anguish.

He took a step forward. 'Is that what this is about?'

'What this is about,' said Pepper through a haze of misery, 'is me. I am who I am. And I sleep alone.'

He stopped as if he had been turned to stone.

She blundered on. 'Look, Steven, I've always known I have a destiny. My career. I don't do relationships. I always knew I couldn't afford to get sidetracked. And I—'

Steven put up a hand. 'No need to say any more.'

'But I want to explain…'

'What's to explain?' His smile was wintry. 'You can't afford to get sidetracked. It's very clear.'

Pepper set her teeth. 'You're not making this easy.'

'Well, excuse me.'

Steven picked up the loaf and, very precisely, threw it straight at the coffee maker. It crashed onto the floor in hail of aromatic liquid and shards of glass.

'Steven!'

'Sorry,' he said, not sounding it. 'Go on. You were saying how hard I'm making it for you to walk out on me.'

She was appalled. What had she done? This is what comes of playing games when you don't know the rules, she scolded herself. But inside she was shaking. The bespattered kitchen looked like a battle ground. She had never been caught in a battle before. Certainly never started it herself.

She said feverishly, 'That's not fair.' But she did not believe it.

Neither did Steven, clearly. 'What is?' he said in a voice

like iron. 'If you're waiting for me to apologise for making love to you, you'll wait for ever.'

'Please—' But no more sound came out.

'Will you tell me one thing?'

She spread her hands, helpless.

'Do all your lovers get their marching orders in the morning?'

Their eyes locked. He looked as if he *hated* her.

Pepper felt her heart contract to dense, cold emptiness. And the fact that it was more than half her fault did not help. That was when she gave up.

She fled.

CHAPTER EIGHT

STEVEN was like a bear with a sore head this morning. Val told him so, indignant.

He smiled, though the smile didn't reach his eyes. 'Missed my run this morning. It's made me ratty. Sorry!'

She accepted his apology. But lack of exercise wasn't at all what had made him ratty, she thought. It was another of those damned demanding women. She could cheerfully have boiled Pepper Calhoun in oil.

It seemed as if every other message this morning was about the woman, too. Martin Tammery had e-mailed Steven a reference to a piece about her company in one of the broadsheet's online editions. There were five separate messages from the office of the President, Calhoun Carter Industries. Steven read them over her shoulder and zapped them immediately, snarling.

And, to crown it all, one of the students invaded the office at the busiest time of the day and Steven, who should have told him to make an appointment and get out, sat on the edge of her desk and swigged coffee with him.

'Debate with Pepper Calhoun?' said Geoff tantalisingly.

Val snorted. They both ignored her.

'She's really nice, isn't she? It would be so cool to have the two of you going head to head.'

Steven winced.

Geoff didn't notice. 'Real crowd-puller,' he said enthusiastically. 'I can get the media on board, too. Do you think she'll do it?'

Not for a moment, thought Steven. He said aloud, 'You'd have to ask her.'

'Okay. And if I do, you're up for it?'

'I'm up for it,' agreed Steven, with a ghost of a smile. 'Let me know what she says.'

But he already knew the most important thing she said. *I sleep alone.* Of course she did. She was the Tiger Cub, with her destiny sorted. There was no room in it for a man with too many responsibilities and a nine-year-old to take care of. Hell, she hadn't even remembered Windflower's name. She was another Courtney.

He had thought she was so different. On the plane she had seemed so natural, sweet-eyed and flustered. It must have been a temporary hitch. Underneath she was not a shy goddess; she was another fully paid-up post feminist juggernaut, determined to have her own way in everything and serenely assured that she was entitled to exactly that. No matter who got hurt.

That brought him to a halt as if he had walked into a wall.

Is that what's wrong, then? Did she hurt me when she walked out this morning? Really? Annoy me, sure. Give my ego a nasty knock, certainly. But *hurt*?

He thought about it. It was true. Even Courtney at her worst had not hurt him like this. Oh, she had tied him up in knots with her eyelashes and touch me, touch me not games. But she had not excavated his heart and then discarded it. Pepper Calhoun had walked out as if love was not worth bothering with in comparison with the great god of commerce! Oh, yes, he was hurt all right.

So what was he going to do about it?

It was a horrible journey back to London. Pepper huddled into the corner of the carriage, trying to make herself invisible.

She went over and over everything Steven had said, everything he had done. How could she ever have called him ungentlemanly? His chivalry brought tears to her eyes. No one would have thought that he was the same man who had said, 'It's a simple equation. If you take in more energy than you use in exercise you store up fat.'

But he was. He could pretend all he liked that he did not notice or did not care. But she was a human potato. Everyone knew that. And he was a man with no patience for excuses.

He had a conscience about what he had said on that hateful television programme; she knew that. So he had decided to give her a perfect day. Hell, he had even told her as much. Clearly he thought that the perfect day for a female geek like her should culminate in a spot of romancing in the rose garden followed by bed.

And he was right. Perfect just about covered it.

He was kind. He was masterly. He made her laugh—and he had made her forget, for a while at least, that romance in the rose garden was not her scene. She might well have fallen in love with a genius. But the genius had just been trying to give her a day to remember.

'Reality check,' said Pepper aloud in the empty carriage. 'He's a contender. You're not. In fact, face it, on the dating track you're a non-starter. Time to wake up, Pepper Calhoun.'

There was nobody home when Pepper let herself into the apartment. It was a relief. She looked a disaster, and not just because she was wearing yesterday's suit.

She got under the shower and let it drum on her skin until she was pink all over and her eyes were watering from the shower gel. Or the spray. Or anything but silly tears.

You inspire me. Well, how ludicrous was that? You would have to be amazingly naïve to believe a man who said stuff like that. Naïve and gullible and— Desperate?

'I need to work,' Pepper said loudly.

She dressed in a fresh business suit, over a blouse of eye-hurting whiteness, and went out to harass a startled designer. When she could no longer think of anything to discuss with the young design team she went into an art gallery and glared so hard at the paintings on display that the gallery staff breathed a sigh of relief when she left.

The hot day declined into a muggy evening. The sky was savage, with great streaks of orange, heralding another wonderful summer day tomorrow. It reminded all too vividly her of that brilliant sunrise on the plane. Then she had thought the worst of her problems was her grandmother. Huh!

Pepper sniffed hard and stopped at a kiosk to buy some cheap sunglasses. No need to look at the damned sunset if she didn't want to! She bought a pocket-size pack of paper tissues as well, and blew her nose with violence.

Then she marched home, beside the gleaming river, oblivious to the traffic that roared at her shoulder. Oblivious to everything, in fact, until her feet reminded her that her elegant shoes were not designed for long-distance walking.

Hot and blistered and breathing hard, Pepper faced a series of nasty truths. She had been letting herself off for too long. But she was too heavy for her own health or her peace of mind. And Steven was right. She could do something about it if she wanted to.

'I want to,' said Pepper aloud. 'I *need* to.'

She needed to be sure there would be no more nights lying awake trying to forget that she hated herself. No more mornings trying to pretend it did not matter. Above all, no more gorgeous men thinking they had to be kind to her.

'What I need,' she told the river blackly, 'is a life strategy. And some decent walking shoes.'

In the end, she padded over the Albert Bridge in the gathering twilight with her shoes in her hand.

Both cousins came out of the kitchen to greet her as she let herself into the apartment and limped down the hallway. Suddenly she saw the downside of communal living.

'What?' said Pepper pugnaciously.

The first person to ask if she had been crying was asking for *death*.

Izzy said, 'Oh, boy, have you stirred up Oxford.'

'What?'

'The machine is blocked with messages.' Jemima was not best pleased. She was usually the one with the high telephone hit rate. 'Mainly the hunk with the eyebrows. Also his secretary, a moppet who says she's his niece, and some student you threw darts at last night.'

'*What?*'

Izzy dug Jemima in the ribs. 'Don't be mischievous.' And, to Pepper, 'He says he met you last night playing darts. Geoff Someone. He wants you to take part in a debate that some college is going to run to raise funds. He left a number.'

'They all left a number.' Jemima was unforgiving. 'The *same* number.'

'No, be fair, Jay Jay. The student's number was different.' She looked at Pepper with deep amusement. 'Men are always wrong, eh? What *have* you been up to?'

Pepper went scarlet. But she was still fighting her corner. 'I don't know what you mean,' she said with spirit.

'That's what they want to debate. Men are always wrong. You're apparently first choice to propose the motion. Who did you take to pieces last night?'

'I wish,' muttered Pepper. She stamped off to her room before they could demand an explanation.

She threw away the ruined tights and plastered her blisters. Then she awarded herself her second prolonged shower of the day. It gave her valuable thinking time. Emerging with newly washed hair and a point by point programme for the rest of her life strategy, she took up her stand in the doorway of the main room and made a public announcement.

'I am going on a health programme.'

The other two stared.

'I have been sitting in front of a computer for too long. I've got into the habit, but I can change. I can think and walk, after all. I don't have to be this unfit. And I certainly don't have to be this heavy. I am going to do something about it.'

They were not as enthusiastic as she expected.

'Oh?' said Jemima coldly. 'Well, good luck.'

And Izzy didn't say anything at all.

'Gee, thanks for the support,' said Pepper dryly.

But it didn't make any difference. She was still going to

do it. She did not return any of the phone calls and she did not do any more work on her project. She spent the rest of the evening researching options on the Internet.

So when Izzy came into her bedroom and said, 'The hunk is on the phone again,' she barely looked up from the screen.

'Tell him I've gone to the moon.'

Izzy passed her the handset. 'Tell him yourself.' She walked out before Pepper could pass the telephone right back.

Damn!

'What is it?' said Pepper into the handset cautiously.

His voice was very cool, very professional. 'We need to meet.'

Don't be kind to me, cried her heart. Aloud she said, 'No, we don't.'

'Oh, but we do.' There was amusement there. 'You've left an incendiary tee shirt here. I need to give it back.'

'Post it,' she said curtly.

'And I'd like to continue our discussion. Your grandmother has been in touch.'

'*What?*'

'So I thought we might have a talk about this business destiny of yours. Having spoken to her, I can't believe that you take that woman's claptrap seriously.'

Pepper shut her eyes. Just for a moment she let herself play with the fantasy of lying in his arms in front of the fire in the Master's Lodgings, just talking and teasing and— Stop it, she thought. That's not for you.

She drew a deep, steadying breath and told him the truth.

'Discussion won't change a thing, Steven. I made my choices a long time ago.'

'I don't accept that. You can change—'

'Yes, but I haven't,' she interrupted. 'I'm still the same person—too serious, too uncool.' She swallowed. 'Too heavy.'

There was absolute silence at the other end of the line. Now, if ever, was the time for him to leap in with denials.

He didn't. Pepper pressed her lips together until they were bloodless.

'So, please—don't call me again,' she said steadily. 'I really would rather get on with my life.'

CHAPTER NINE

STEVEN put the phone down and stared out at the Master's Garden. A couple of his senior colleagues were escorting a party among the tangled roses in the evening shadows but he did not see them. All he could see was Pepper, with pollen on her nose and sequins on her bosom, spelling out 'Go for it' in pouting bravura.

'*Yes!*' he said triumphantly.

He had been right after all. She was everything he had first thought. Shy and flustered and clever and natural and—adorable. And absolutely daft about her body. But he could deal with that.

'Nobody better,' Steven said with a wicked grin.

Too heavy, forsooth! The woman needed some serious re-education. And Steven Konig had been a chemist specialising in food substitutes when he'd set up Kplant. If anyone knew just where to look for the evidence it was Steven. Pepper Calhoun would not know what had hit her.

Having established her new life strategy, Pepper embarked on it the very next day. She called a counsellor and signed up to a programme that combined group therapy with a practical approach to food issues. She also signed the lease on some office space and bought some walking shoes.

'From now on I walk to work,' she announced to the cousins. 'Whatever goes wrong in my life from now on, it's not going to be because I feel disgusting.'

'Good for you,' said Izzy.

Jemima got up and walked out of the sitting room. Pepper raised her eyebrows.

'Competitive dieter,' said Izzy dismissively. 'Forget it. What's your target?'

'No target,' said Pepper, who had taken careful notes during her conversation with her counsellor. 'I just want to feel better.'

She did not say, and Izzy did not seem to guess, that getting over Steven Konig would be a good first step.

Fortunately, she did not have the chance to think much about him in the next couple of days. Building work started on the first shop, and she wanted to be on site at least once a day. Added to that, the proofs of the first catalogue were coming through and there was a steady trickle of enquiries from the media. Pepper was working an eighteen-hour day and grateful for it.

She thought that Steven had wiped her out of his memory. She tried to be grateful for that, too. She certainly convinced herself that it was for the best. Well, in the long term, anyway.

And then she saw a message from him when she opened up her e-mail one morning. She made a sound between a bat squeak and a strangled gurgle and froze. Like a robot, she opened the message.

It was brief. And clear. And impersonal.

And *crazy*.

It was headed 'Real American Woman', and it said:

The ideal American woman is five feet seven inches, weighs 110 pounds and wears a size four; the REAL American woman is five feet four inches, weighs 144 pounds and wears a size twelve. (Fraser, 1997, Food Angst: The Diet Trap. *Family Therapy Networker*, pp. 44+.)

He had rounded it off with a little message of his own:

Clear? S.

Pepper choked.

'What is it?' said Izzy, installed on the other side of the desk.

'I think Steven Konig has just told me not to make a fuss about nothing,' said Pepper in a stunned voice.

Izzy got up and strolled round to take a look at the e-mail. She read it and grinned. 'You could be right. Good for the hunk.'

The messages continued.

'I don't believe it,' said Pepper, flustered. 'He's gone on a Make Pepper Feel Good About Herself campaign. Every morning I open my e-mail and there's another piece from some scientific journal or other.'

'He certainly knows how to get your attention,' said Izzy. She approved of Steven Konig more and more. 'No declarations. He knows you wouldn't believe them. So he sticks to well-researched findings until you can't argue and then— whoosh!' And she did that exploding firework thing with her hands again.

Pepper swallowed. 'Declarations?' she said uncertainly.

Izzy was maddeningly smug. 'Smooth. Very smooth.' And she refused to be drawn further.

Steven himself stayed an unseen, unheard, unforgettable presence.

'Why doesn't he call me and get it over with?' said Pepper aloud, frustrated.

But she herself had told him not to. So of course he wouldn't. This was a man of old-fashioned chivalry.

His chivalry sent her round the park on a daily power walk, stamping out her bewildered irritation on the grass.

Then one night at Soup Group she heard herself pour it all out. Her fellow group members were interested, entertained, and not entirely on her side.

'Give the guy a break,' said one of them, summing up the feeling of the meeting. 'Call him. You know you want to.'

She did. Pepper was honest enough to admit that. And that daily bombardment of learned papers on weight and nutrition was making her suspect that Steven wanted it, too. Really wanted it, rather than just being kind.

The day came when she agreed to the final proof of the catalogue. The builders more or less threw her off the shop site bodily. Izzy had taken charge of arranging warehousing for the first shipments of clothes which were beginning to come in. There was not a thing she could find to do.

You've run out of displacement activity, Pepper told herself. So why put it off any longer?

She called Queen Margaret's College and got the disapproving secretary.

No, the Master was not available. The Master was at a meeting of the Funding Committee and would not be free for the rest of the day. His diary was full until the end of the week. She could—without enthusiasm—take a message.

Deflated, Pepper left her name and number and rang off. She was prowling restlessly round the office when the doorbell rang. She looked at the street camera and froze in amazement. It was Mary Ellen Calhoun.

She buzzed her in, then went onto the landing to meet her. What on earth did her grandmother want? She had not tried to make contact since that day she'd thrown Pepper out of the Calhoun building.

Mary Ellen's first words were typical. 'That elevator is too old. Makes investors think you're cutting corners.'

'Not at all,' said Pepper composedly. 'This is Britain, Grandma. The investors take one look at all that Edwardian metalwork and decide we've got class.' She did not offer to kiss Mary Ellen but held open the door to the office. 'Welcome. Come in.'

Mary Ellen stripped off her gloves, looking round her critically. 'You gave up Calhoun Carter for *this*?'

'Looks like it. Can I get you a coffee?'

Mary Ellen went over to the big rooftop window and looked out across the Victorian chimneys. 'Haven't you even got a PA?' she said over her shoulder.

'She's out at the warehouse.'

Pepper poured coffee as she knew her grandmother liked it—black with four spoons of sugar—and took it across to her. Even Mary Ellen wouldn't be able to fault their stylish china, she thought with relief.

'Sit?'

'I'm not staying. This won't take long.'

Mary Ellen did not look very forgiving. Pepper braced herself.

'I saw the report of your company launch. Clever.'

'I didn't use the Calhoun name,' Pepper said quickly, before her grandmother could accuse her.

Mary Ellen gave a wintry smile. 'So I saw. I admit this *Attic* thing of yours looks like a good idea. I've come to offer a trade.'

Pepper frowned. Her grandmother was always at her most dangerous when she sounded reasonable.

'What sort of trade?'

'You come back to Calhoun Carter and you can bring this little project of yours with you. We'll capitalise it properly. You retain an advisory role, of course.'

Pepper laughed aloud. 'You don't change, do you, Grandma? No thanks. I don't want an advisory role. I want to work on my own idea and see where it takes me. But thank you for the offer. Now, how have you been?'

Mary Ellen put down her coffee. 'Are you serious about him?'

Pepper blinked. 'What?'

'This Oxford guy.'

'*What?*'

'You are such a *child*,' said Mary Ellen with concentrated venom. 'You think you only have to get a crush on someone and he falls into your arms. That's soap opera. The real world doesn't work like that.'

Pepper blinked. 'I don't know what you're talking about.'

'He e-mailed the company looking for you, you know. Weeks ago. Why would he have done that if he didn't know you were my heir?'

Suddenly Pepper felt sorry for her. She said gently, 'If you're talking about Steven Konig, I don't think my relationship with him is any of your business.'

Mary Ellen snorted. 'It's my business if I'm going to have to pay the bill. How much is he going to cost me?'

Pepper laughed aloud. Mary Ellen was so affronted she forgot to keep her jaw rigid and a thousand age lines appeared under her elaborate make-up. She said furiously, 'Don't you laugh. Don't you dare laugh. I've always given you what you wanted.'

'No, Grandma.' Pepper brought her laughter under control but she spoke gently. 'You've given me what *you* wanted. And, believe me, I don't want you to buy me a man. And even if I did, Steven Konig isn't for sale.'

'Everyone is for sale. It's just a question of the price.'

Pepper shook her head. 'You know, I'm sorry for you if that's really the way you feel.'

Something exploded in her grandmother. 'You think you can get him on your own? Really? How? You're not a proper woman. You're a schoolgirl who thinks she has learned to play with the grown-ups. You have no charm. You're overweight. You don't know how to talk to a man. And this Konig is a very successful man, by what I hear. Attractive, too. You haven't a hope.'

Pepper thought of all his daily educational e-mails and bit back a smile.

'You could just be wrong there, Grandma,' she said. And found she believed it.

Mary Ellen had a lot more to say but Pepper wasn't listening. *She believed it.* Steven wanted her for herself. She was sure of it. And it was up to her to make the next move. Wimpy telephone calls wouldn't do the business. She had to be pro-active.

'Sorry to hurry you along, Grandma. But I've got a lot to do.' She gave her grandmother her gloves and virtually hustled her out of the office, just remembering to ask which hotel she was staying at before she closed the elevator grille on her. 'Goodbye.'

She made her arrangements fast, starting with a hired limousine to take her to Oxford. Pepper had learned to economise in the last three months. But this was no time to be penny-pinching. This was her life on the line.

'This is so cool,' said Geoff, meeting her at the porter's lodge.

Pepper quelled a flutter of alarm. It had been her idea after all. 'I hope so,' she said calmly.

'It'll be, like, total gasp time.'

'You haven't told anyone?'

He grinned. 'No one. Not even the guy I told to bring his camera in to hall. He thinks there's going to be a bread roll throwing match before dinner or something.' He hugged himself. 'This is going to get so many column inches.'

'Er—yes.' Pepper knew it was true. It was partly why she had thought of doing this in the first place, after all. But she still didn't like to think about it too closely.

'You need to change your gear?'

Her chin went up. Part of her preparations had been to buy a dress that made her eyes water just to look at. She gave thanks for Soup Group. Not so much that she had lost a huge amount of weight. But she had found the confidence to wear something like that.

She swallowed. 'Yes.'

'You can use my room. There's half an hour before formal hall. I've done a deal with a guy who had signed in his girlfriend, so there's room for you but you're not actually on the guest list by name.' His grin stretched from ear to ear. 'King Kong is going to be utterly blown away when he sees you.'

Pepper permitted herself a small sedate smile. 'I certainly hope so. That's the object of the exercise, after all.'

CHAPTER TEN

THE dress was an adventure all on its own. For a woman who normally dressed in severe business suits and neat collared blouses, ankle-length silk would have been adventure enough. But, in addition, this dress was all the colours red: from nearly purple wine through heart-of-the-fire scarlet to a brilliant and blinding cerise.

'It's not a dress for a redhead,' Pepper had said, taken aback when Izzy had first seized it out of the young designer's first delivery.

'It's a dress for anyone who is woman enough to wear it,' Izzy said firmly.

And when Pepper tried it on she saw what she meant. It was not particularly close fitting, but the silk flowed like water, setting the reds into a ripple like spilled wine, like sunset. Or sunrise, thought Pepper, remembering piratically strong arms and a sunrise zipping up from the horizon towards them at delirious speed. She had lost her balance then—had she ever really recovered it? She shivered—and knew in that moment that she and the dress were made for each other.

'I'll take it. Tell Eva we'll need a replacement,' she said.

Izzy swept her credit card through their previously untouched machine. Then they stood up and solemnly toasted *Out of the Attic's* first sale.

And now here she was, on a summer evening, walking round a quad that had not changed in four centuries, with her shoulders bare to the evening breeze, her hands in crimson gloves to the elbow, her hair loosely piled on top of her head and every single eye on her flame dress.

Pepper lifted her chin. 'I can do this.'

'Sure you can,' said Geoff, brimming with excitement.

174

He was so overcome by the momentousness of the encounter he was about to engineer that he had changed into a tuxedo, to Pepper's amazement. So had all his friends. She went into her first dinner at Queen Margaret's College surrounded by a phalanx of formally dressed young men.

They had clearly planned it carefully, seating her on one of the polished wooden benches at the far end of one of the gleaming refectory tables. Steven would be sitting at High Table, with the college dignitaries and their guests, they told her. Often he missed, but tonight he had to be present. The external members of the Fund-Raising Committee always expected a full college dinner for their trouble and he was their host.

Pepper moistened her lips nervously as the college servants lit branches of candles in the middle of the tables. To her, the whole scene looked like something out of a fairy story: the formally dressed men, the glint of candlelight on wood and silver and wine, the evening sun through tall stained glass windows. But her companions were happily discussing computer games as if this was a perfectly ordinary way to take your evening meal.

'All it needs is minstrels,' muttered Pepper.

Geoff broke off his conversation, mock reproachful. 'Well, if you give me more than four hours' notice next time, I'll do my best.'

She looked round, hoping that her assumed mockery disguised the fact that she was shaking to her strappy shoes. 'It's archaic.'

'It's tradition.'

And then a gong sounded, and there was a scraping of benches as everyone stood up and the High Table party came in. They were all wearing academic gowns. It made them look like a convention of wizards, thought Pepper, getting jumpier by the minute.

Steven looked particularly wizardly, remote and unapproachable in his black robe. No sign of the pirate now. He looked as if the weight of the world rested on his shoulders.

There was a brief Latin grace, then everyone sat down and the buzz started again.

'Looks like the fund-raisers gave Kong a bad time,' someone said across the table to Geoff.

'Then he's in luck,' said Geoff cheerfully. 'We're going to help him out. Right, Pepper?'

She swallowed. 'Here comes the cavalry,' she agreed.

The meal was no doubt delicious. Pepper did not eat a mouthful—and it had nothing to do with her health programme. By the time the port was introduced her throat was as dry as brick dust and she was beginning to twitch with untapped adrenaline.

'How much longer?' she muttered to Geoff.

He pursed his lips, looking round the room. The candles were more than half burned down. Already a couple of people had approached the dais, bowed to the Master and left the dining hall. Soon the occasion would be drawing to a close; even Pepper could see that.

Geoff shrugged. 'Any time you like.'

Her stomach slid away from her. She moistened her lips, drew a deep breath and got to her feet.

At first the looks were curious, no more than that. Pepper was nothing special. Every woman in the room had dressed elegantly. But, as she walked slowly towards the dais, the diners realised three things: they had never seen her in college before; she did not look like a student; and Steven Konig was staring at her mesmerised. The buzz in the hall fell almost to silence.

Pepper felt her colour rise. And she still had half that damned slippery floor to cover. Don't let me skid in these crazy shoes, she prayed.

It did not show. She walked on as steadily as a young judge until she got to the dais. There, instead of standing in the body of the hall and bowing modestly to be excused, she went up the four steps and stood in front of the Master's chair, with the gleaming table between them.

Slowly, he got to his feet. In perfect silence he stood there, staring at her. The buzz quietened to perfect silence.

Pepper stripped off her right glove and laid it carefully down on the table.

'A challenge, Master,' she said formally. 'A debate in this hall. Men are always wrong.'

Steven's eyes bored into hers as if they were alone. Pepper felt the colour rise in her cheeks and was furious with herself. And him. He was not supposed to stand there glaring at her. He was supposed to accept the challenge. Then everyone could go off to call the gossip columns. But he did not. He just looked and looked as if he was never going to speak again.

Pepper set her jaw. 'Wh-what do you say?'

'What?' He sounded distracted. And he was looking at her as if he wanted to slip those damned straps off and...

Pepper felt as if she were one huge blush. She squared her shoulders and said loudly, 'A public debate. Entrance admission to go to the College Repairs Fund. You and me.'

The fund-raisers began to realise what this was about. They started to look at each other, instead of her and Steven. There was the beginning of an approving buzz along High Table.

A pleasant-faced elderly man leaned forward across a couple of the guests to address Steven, smiling.

'I urge you to accept, Master. Honour of the college and all that.'

At last Steven came out of his trance. 'Thank you for your advice, Dean. Excellent as always.' He made Pepper a little bow. 'I accept with pleasure, Ms Calhoun.'

There was a roar of delight from the body of the hall. Spontaneous clapping broke out.

Pepper dipped her head, shy now that her task was accomplished. Negotiating skirt and slender-heeled shoes carefully on that lethal floor, she turned, not realising that Steven was coming rapidly round the table to her. At least, she didn't realise it until she found her hand taken.

'Allow me,' said Steven.

His voice sounded odd. She looked up unwisely and her shoe skidded.

He caught her. Of course he caught her. Didn't he always? He had a knack for it, Pepper thought hazily. She clutched at his arm and just about stayed upright. But her heart lurched like crazy when she saw the look in his eyes.

'This is where I came in, I think,' he said, laughing down at her.

He walked her straight out through the murmuring crowd in the candlelit hall and she didn't see a single face as they went.

No garden interlude this evening. He took her straight to his rooms and shut the door against the world.

'Now—that challenge,' he murmured gently.

And took her in his arms, not gently at all.

When he raised his head he looked shaken. 'I knew it,' he said.

'Wha—?' said Pepper, still dazed and not too steady on her smart shoes.

'I'm in love with you,' said Steven baldly.

Pepper blinked. 'You don't sound very happy about it,' she said, torn between amusement and hurt.

'I'm not.' He put her away from him. 'You'd better know the whole truth,' he said harshly. 'The last time I was in love I got burned. Badly. You've already felt the backlash from that, I'm afraid.'

Pepper kicked off her shoes. It was easier, and anyway it made her feel more at home among his things. She sank onto an elderly sofa and pulled her feet up under her skirt.

'Courtney?' she asked.

He was startled. 'Someone's been talking?'

She shook her head. 'You mentioned her once.' She said with difficulty, 'I paid attention. It seemed important.'

He seized her hand and squeezed it so hard that she felt her bones would crack. But she did not cry out.

'Yes. Yes, it was.' He sounded shaken. 'It's a classic. I

had a good friend—my best friend, like a brother. Courtney decided she wanted him instead.' He looked away. 'Well, not instead, actually. As well. She thought I was so besotted that I'd be there to cheat on my friend whenever she wanted a little fun on the side.'

Pepper was so angry that she could have smashed Courtney through one of the long windows, if the woman had been in the room with them.

Instead she said, 'She didn't know you very well.'

He gave a shaken laugh and the grip on her fingers relaxed. 'You're right. She didn't.'

'So what happened to her? Is she still around?'

'In a way. She is Windflower's mother.'

Pepper digested that. 'I *see*. So Jan—er—Windflower is the daughter of this almost brother of yours?'

He nodded. 'His parents were like a second family to me when my father died. And Tom made Windflower my god-daughter. I couldn't turn my back on her.'

Pepper frowned. 'Of course you couldn't.'

Steven said, in an oddly warning voice, 'I think she'll be with me a long time. Her mother is off finding herself some-where.'

'That's tough,' said Pepper.

'Then—you don't mind?'

She was bewildered. 'Mind?'

'I thought you hated my having a child around. Especially the daughter of an old girlfriend.'

'"Hated"—' She shook her head. 'I've missed something somewhere. Where did that come from?'

Steven let go her hand. 'You couldn't even remember her name,' he said quietly. 'I took that as a pretty clear indicator that you wished she wasn't around.'

Pepper bounced off the sofa. 'Oh, that's stupid. I couldn't remember her name because I think of her as Janice.'

It was Steven's turn for bewilderment. He gaped.

'*Janice?*'

'That's what she told me she was called,' said Pepper

crisply. 'At Indigo. While she was giving me some free advice on make-up. At the time, something told me she was lying. But I never dreamed her name was anything so awful. Windflower—poor child.'

Steven began to laugh. He laughed until he could not speak. In the end he sank onto the sofa and took her with him in a flurry of firelight silk and bare feet.

'So you're not jealous of Courtney?'

'Huh!'

'I won't pretend,' he said gravely. 'She used to bring me out in a cold sweat every time I looked at her.'

Pepper took his face between her hands and looked at him soberly. 'And she asked you to cheat on your friend. She blew her chances a long time ago.'

'Yes,' said Steven on a long note of discovery. 'Yes, she did.' He feathered a kiss across her mouth. 'But she never got to me the way you do.'

'Ah.' Pepper found she couldn't meet his eyes. Which was crazy, really. But—she couldn't. 'Look,' she said, trying to tell the truth, 'I'm very flattered but—'

'But you don't trust me.'

He sounded surprisingly calm about it. She dared a quick look at him, found that he was looking at her in a way that made her head swim, and decided it was prudent to transfer her gaze to his rusty black robe. He looked every inch the Master in his academic dress. He had no right to be looking at her in that way.

Pepper shook her head. 'I don't have very good experience of trusting people,' she said with wincing honesty. 'You had your Courtney. Well, I had my own disasters. I discovered— rather late—that my dates have been organised by my grandmother all my life.'

Steven searched her face. 'I don't understand.'

She explained about Ed Ivanov in a cool, neutral voice. 'And I gather that he wasn't the only one. Only I didn't know it. I thought he liked me. Hell, I even thought my grandmother liked me,' she said on a little surge of self-contempt. 'How stupid can you be?'

'Meaning?' His voice was clipped.

She shut her eyes for a moment. 'I wish I were like my cousins. They know what they're doing with relationships.' She fought tears and won. She opened her eyes and said baldly, 'I don't.'

There was silence while he digested that. 'Translation, please,' he said at last, still clipped.

She floundered. 'When we—when I—that day—'

'Our perfect day?'

She smiled faintly. 'That day, yes. I'd never done anything like that before.'

There was a glimmer under the ice. 'That makes two of us.'

That startled her into meeting his eyes at last. 'Really?'

'Are you—?' He had gone all British and clipped. It was surprisingly frightening. 'Are you *daring* to think that I make a habit of taking days off at the drop of a hat, just to take stroppy women on the river?'

Pepper reminded herself that she had bested a woman who terrified a workforce of a hundred thousand. She stuck her chin in the air.

'I don't know what you did before you met me,' she said loftily.

He gave a sudden bark of laughter. 'Stayed sane,' he said. 'Stop tormenting me, you crazy woman. Are you going to marry me or not?'

She did not believe he had said that. She stared at him, eyes wide and vulnerable, utterly silenced.

Steven groaned. 'Or do I have to ask you again in the middle of that damned debate of yours?'

Pepper said slowly, 'Would you?'

'If I have to, yes.'

'But you'd hate it.'

He interrupted. 'I've declared myself to your gorgon of a

grandmother. The whole of Oxford will be a piece of cake by comparison.'

She was instantly ice. 'You've spoken to my grandmother?'

Steven stayed calm. 'I sent an e-mail to her company when I was trying to track you down.' He added patiently, 'You'd gone to ground. I didn't have many clues. God knows what brought her up from the black lagoon this week. But she dropped by to suggest I could make a tidy sum if I persuaded you to go back to the States.' Pepper thought of what Mary Ellen had said only this afternoon.

She said slowly, 'She implied that she would pay you to marry me?'

Steven shuddered. 'Shrewd, as I'd already told her that I was going to ask you. Now, that is a woman who could give classes in Control Freakery.'

'You'd already told her—'

'Just before I threw her out, yes.'

Pepper felt terribly humble. Yet proud at the same time. And desperately uncertain, as if it was bad luck to believe that so much happiness could come all at once. Mary Ellen's poisonous words still echoed: 'You have no charm. You're overweight. You haven't a hope.'

Steven stood up suddenly. Reaching out, he brought her to her feet and looked at her very steadily.

'Penelope Anne Calhoun, you are a woman I did not believe could exist. You are natural and bright and funny and you've had my heart on a stick since the first time you fell into my arms. For God's sake, marry me and give me back my sanity.'

But still she hesitated.

He groaned. 'Pepper, for God's sake. I love you. What more can I say? Or—don't you love me, after all?'

'Mary Ellen said I was a potato,' she said in a final rush of wincing honesty.

There was an incredulous silence.

Then Steven sighed. 'I wish you wouldn't think of yourself

like that,' he said, irritated. 'Think of yourself as lavish. Abundant. Didn't I read that Arab princes are always attracted to plump ladies to prove how rich they are?'

She could not have been more startled if he had suddenly stood on his head in front of her. Years of pain disappeared like fog in the morning.

Pepper laughed aloud in pure amusement. 'I can see it now.' She struck an attitude. 'The night is young and you're enormous! Very sexy. Not.'

But Steven was taking off his robe, looking thoughtful. 'Rubens' women were pretty damned sexy.'

'But not—'

His jacket followed. 'And you're right. The night is young.'

'Oh,' said Pepper, suddenly very conscious of her bare shoulders and the warmth in his eyes.

'Since you can't make up your mind, I'm going to do something that I've wanted to do all my life,' said Steven with resolution.

'What—?' She broke off. *'Steven!'*

For he had swept her off her feet and draped her over his shoulder as if she were a piece of pirate's booty.

'Captain Blood, my boyhood hero,' he said wickedly.

And carried her up the spiral staircase to bed.

EPILOGUE

THE debate was a huge success. The dining room was full to overflowing. The speeches were witty and pertinent and widely reported. An old alumnus undertook to pay for the repairs to the roof. Various college funds were boosted to a healthier level than they had ever been in the whole of their existence. Even the Dean said that Steven Konig had proved his worth. At last he had succeed in raising the college's profile.

Of course, the news that he was going to marry up-and-coming retail entrepreneur Pepper Calhoun didn't hurt. Though the Dean wished he wouldn't hold hands with her in public.

Pepper did not care. Steven reached for her whenever they were close enough to touch. He was unashamed about it. And so, slowly, she learned to reach for him, too.

On the day that they finally told the world they were going to marry they were sitting in the middle of a newly mown meadow. She was leaning against his shoulder, basking in sun and the smell of fresh-cut grass.

Windflower was with them for a picnic, having agreed to fit them into her social calendar for once. They wanted to tell her first.

She considered them both gravely, then turned her attention to Pepper. 'Do you know lots and lots about children?' she said with reserve.

Pepper was alarmed. 'Not a thing.' A thought struck her and she gave a spurt of laughter. 'Heck, I wasn't much of a child myself, now I come to think of it. I have a lot to learn.'

Windflower sucked her teeth. Pepper looked anxiously at

Steven. He shook his head in silent caution. She turned back to Windflower.

'Will that be a problem?'

Windflower took a considered decision.

'Never mind. Uncle Steven and I will teach you,' she said kindly.

'Thank you,' said Pepper with real gratitude.

Windflower was magnanimous. 'No problem.'

She pottered off to play cricket with some children she had already identified further down the riverbank. They watched her go with resignation.

'Do you think she's okay with this really?' asked Pepper, still anxious.

'I think she's still working on a change of name,' said Steven callously. 'I'm just waiting for her to suggest it as part of our wedding celebrations.'

Pepper gave a choke of laughter. 'Well, why not? Everything else is changing.'

He held her close. 'Isn't it just? A few months ago I was a man without a family or even a private life. And now—'

'And now you're a man just loaded down with domestic responsibilities,' she teased him.

Steven took her hand and carried it to his lips. His look was heart-stoppingly tender.

'No, sweetheart,' he said softly. 'Now I'm a man in love.'

THE AUSTRALIANS

MEN WHO TURN YOUR WHOLE WORLD UPSIDE DOWN!

Strong and silent...
Powerful and passionate...
Tough and tender...

Who can resist the rugged loners
of the Outback? As tough and untamed
as the land they rule, they burn as hot as the
Australian sun once they meet the women
they've been waiting for.

HARLEQUIN®
Romance®

is delighted
to present

ACCIDENTAL BRIDE

on-sale June (#3754)

by fresh talent

Darcy Maguire

*And don't miss stories of
seduction and passion by
Australian Harlequin
Presents® authors...*

HARLEQUIN®
Makes any time special®

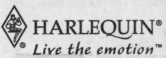

The world's bestselling romance series.

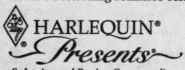

HARLEQUIN®
Presents

Seduction and Passion Guaranteed!

Every book is part of a miniseries in 2003.
These are just some of the exciting themes you can expect...

Your dream ticket to the vacation
of a lifetime!

Tall, dark—and
ready to marry!

They're guaranteed
to raise your pulse!

They're the men who have
everything—except a bride....

Marriage is their mission....

Legally wed, but he's never said,
"I love you..."

They speak the
language of passion

Passion™

Sophisticated spicy stories—
seduction and passion guaranteed

Pick up a Harlequin Presents® novel and you will enter a world
of spine-tingling passion and provocative, tantalizing romance!

Available wherever Harlequin books are sold.

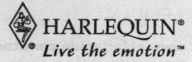

HARLEQUIN®
Live the emotion™

Visit us at www.eHarlequin.com

HPMINP03

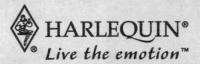